Big Girls Need Love, too! Barbara from Kokomo

Dirk Caldwell Romantic Erotic Novels, Volume 7

Dirk Caldwell

Published by Dirk Caldwell, 2023.

BIG GIRLS NEED LOVE, TOO! BARBARA FROM KOKOMO

First edition. August 11, 2023.

ISBN: 979-8223735816

Written by Dirk Caldwell.

Also by Dirk Caldwell

Adventures of Stan
Stan Does a Big Girl and Gives her a Big Orgasm
Stan Does a Female Police Officer While On Duty
Stan Scores on a Booty Call with Barbara
Stan Takes Barb's Anal Cherry
Stan Teaches Oklahoma Karen About Sex in the City
Stan gets Kinky with Barb on Vacation
Barb Wants more Orgasms with Stan before She gets Engaged to Another Man
Stan Does Barbara's Mom!
Stan Titty Fucks Barbara's Friend!
A Stopover in Eufaula to Fuck Lynn Again
Stan Shows a Redhead How to Have an Orgasm
Liz loses Her Anal Cherry During a Three Way
Stan has Sex with a Black Chick!
Stan Has Sex with a Pregnant Woman!
Stan Sport Fucks a Sexy Lawyer!
Stan Titty Fucks Traci's Grandma!
Stan Titty Fucks His Art Dealer!

Dirk Caldwell Romantic Erotic Novels
A Visit to the Farm with Darla - a Sexy Short Story

A Layover in Omaha with Tina
A Night in Eufaula with Lynn
A Trip to the Lake with Kim
Older Women need Love, too! Erika visits Atlanta
Lessons in Love: Gabriella Visits Indianapolis
Big Girls Need Love, too! Barbara from Kokomo
Flight Attendants want Love: Flying High with Jessica
Back to the Farm with Darla - A Sexy Sequel
Redheads Need Love: Megan From New Orleans
A Big Girl finds Love: Joann from Shreveport
Lust from London: My Affair with a British Nymphomaniac
Paula's Sexy European Weekend
Mother and Daughter Threesome

Dirk Caldwell Sexy Short Stories
To All the Girls I've Loved Before: Sexy Short Stories Book 1
To All the Girls I've Loved Before: Sexy Short Stories Book 2
To All the Girls I've Loved Before: Sexy Short Stories Book 3

Acknowledgment

AI Cover image by Freepik
Back Cover generic airline pilot image by Blake Guidry at unsplash

Introduction

Barbara was on all fours in front of me, her big, ripe, naked body ready for the taking. I admired her big ass and the red marks of our previous activity. Having just finished fucking her pussy from behind while spanking her, she had made the outrageous suggestion that I take her anal cherry. Obligingly, I greased up her asshole and my cock and then pushed the glans against her anus.

"Go ahead!" She exclaimed. "Fuck my ass!"

Encouraged, I eased my rock hard cock forward into her and felt her anal sphincter yield to the pressure of the intruding man meat. Slowly, I entered her ass as she gasped. I had just taken her anal cherry.

My name is Dirk. Well, that's not my real name. I'd never be able to have a normal life if I used my real name. I was an enlisted guy in the Air Force and single at the time of this encounter. I enjoyed being unencumbered and the benefits that came from that. I could travel the world as an international aircrew member and be with any woman I wanted without regret and have always enjoyed the freedom that came with that ability.

I enjoy recalling some of my favorite encounters. Most were great, some were just okay, and some I absolutely could not believe what happened. These are the encounters I write about, as they are the most entertaining and fun to read about. While most of the content in my stories is true, I do spice things up every now and then, but you would be surprised how much happened exactly as written. I've been incredibly lucky with women and am humbled every day that I have had so much success.

As a disclaimer, I always change enough of the information about the ladies so my writing could not possibly be traced back to them. Cities are changed, along with names, occupations, specific characteristics, branches of service for the military, etc. To do otherwise would not be gentlemanly. I do, however, mix in some of my local knowledge about locations. How did I get that information? Let your imagination be your guide.

I hope you enjoy my novels.

Meeting Barb

An Air Force enlisted man in the grade of Staff Sergeant, I was assigned to an air base in Indiana after completing school to be an inflight refueling operator, commonly called boom operator due to the operation of the air refueling 'boom' that I operated to connect two military airplanes in flight. I was a military aircrew member, not a pilot that flew the plane, but an enlisted man that operated the air refueling equipment. I had been in the Air Force for about four years at that point, and after my initial tour as an airplane mechanic, I applied for cross-training to be a boom operator. I was married at the time I applied, but my young wife did not want to leave California where I had served my initial tour. Indiana sounded far away and remote. She wasn't wrong. She left me, and the divorce came through about the time I got to Indiana.

When checking into a new base, there are a myriad of offices to check in with and provide data to. One of these was the base education office that oversaw the many programs to educate military personnel with civilian courses, and also to process the paperwork for the military tuition assistance program. I had adopted a posture of being friendly and flirty with every female I met, with the goal of getting them into bed. At the education office, I kept up the routine and got a response from Barbara, a civil service employee. She was a big girl; much heavier than any woman I had ever been with. I flirted with her and followed up after a few days. She was appreciative of the attention paid to her and invited me to her house for dinner. I accepted and found myself at a small house in Kokomo, Indiana with Barb (Only my Mom calls me Barbara) and her young son, having a wonderful lasagna dinner.

We enjoyed the dinner and the wine that I had brought. Barb was a good cook and a great hostess. At the appropriate time, Barb put her son to bed, and we moved to the living room sofa to watch TV. After a while, I squirmed a little to ease the pressure on my back, which was acting up, likely due to wearing a heavy parachute while lying on my stomach performing air refueling duty. She noticed my discomfort and asked what was wrong, so I told her that I had some back discomfort. She offered to rub my back, which I readily agreed to. I had tried this tactic in my teen years, thinking if I could get a female to rub my bare back, they would be consumed with desire and let me ravish them. It had never worked yet.

I removed my shirt and lay on my stomach on the sofa, with Barb straddling my hips and providing a nice back massage. It was very soothing and pleasing. After a while, I said I was ready to turn over, and she indicated that she was ready to do so.

Changing Positions

I rolled over onto my back with Barb still straddling me. She smiled down at me as she leaned forward and braced herself on my shoulders. Then she leaned in and kissed me. While she was doing that, I took the opportunity to slide my hands under her slacks and panties and fondle her ass. She seemed appreciative, as she sat up, still smiling, and said, "Let's go to the bedroom."

These were the words that every 25-year-old male wanted to hear in this situation. The tactic had finally worked! She swung her legs over me and got up, and I followed her to the bedroom, which was actually just an open area around a dividing wall from the living room. Maybe at one time, it had been a dining room. I had seen the bed when walking to the kitchen for dinner, and again when we went to the living room after, but it did not register at the time. It certainly made the transition from TV watching to getting ready for sex easy.

She went to the far side of the bed and got her clothes off in about 15 seconds, while I was still struggling to get my shoes, socks, pants, and underwear off. Barb did not mess around. She lit a candle on each side of the bed before she lay down and turned off the bedside lamp. She lay on the bed on her side facing me, still with a nice smile. I smiled back as I tore my clothes off, then joined her on the bed on my side, facing her. She reached out and wrapped one hand around my limp cock, not stroking, or pumping. Just holding it. I was wishing it had been erect so she had something solid to hang onto.

I took stock of the naked woman in front of me. Her age was in the low 30s. She had black hair coifed and not below her neck. Her shoulders were rounded up toward her neck as some big women have, and her face was fleshy but not overly so. She was still attractive. Brown eyes under trimmed brows, cheeks just chubby enough, a few smile lines around her mouth, nice even teeth. The usual eye makeup. Lipstick with a red tint. Some fleshiness under her chin. Her neck had some extra flesh, not terrible. My eyes went to her chest. She had big boobs with nice pink nipples. The boobs hung down a bit as would be expected on heavier women. Her stomach was big but not huge, with some stretch marks and a roll where her belt had been a few minutes ago. Her hips were wide, and her ass was well-padded. There was a nice patch of shiny black pubic hair around her pussy. Her labia were thick and meaty. The thighs were big and smooth, knees a bit fleshy, and calves and ankles about the right size as the rest of her. She was a big girl.

A big horny girl as it turned out. She scooted closer to me and looked at me expectantly. I was a 25-year-old novice. I went for the boobs first and started fondling them. She did not seem to mind. I went with kissing each boob and nipple in turn, which seemed like the right thing to do. She still had a hand holding my dick. Maybe she was wanting to feel it transition from flaccid to hard. It was still pretty limp. I had that problem with new women back then. It just needed waking up.

I was caressing her all over by now, running my hands all over, exploring her. Her textures and feel were totally different from my ex-wife, who was the last person I had sex with. I was in an acclimatization period. She had taken to caressing me as well, which was nice. I stroked the inside of her thighs and moved my finger up and down her labia and ran my fingers through her pubic hair. It all felt nice. She moaned a little as my fingers touched the labia. I was learning how to do this, so I tried putting a fingertip between the lips and started gently going up and down the slit. She liked that and moaned a little while her hips squirmed a bit. This was positive feedback, so I felt that I must be doing something right.

In the meantime, my dick was just lying there asleep. I tried more boob fondling and nipple kissing, while I ran my finger up and down her slit. She liked it, I liked it, but my weenie was out for lunch. After a few minutes, I asked her to stroke me, and she did. The weenie liked that and got sort of stiff after a few minutes. I put my finger into her vaginal vault hole, and she shuddered and moaned. All good reactions. Then she said something odd.

"I have several small orgasms during sex. That was the first one, thanks!"

What's a guy to say? You're welcome. I smiled at her and kissed her again while keeping up the fingering. My dick was almost in a usable state, so I rolled her onto her back and crouched between her legs, putting the head of my cock up against her labia. My ex always wanted to guide it in, would all women do that? Barb got the hint and gently put me at the door to heaven. I pushed in a little, felt my glans clear the outer labia, then I felt a big nothing. I mean, it was wet, warm, and pleasant but did not feel like any pussy I had ever been in. There was no feeling of friction, no encasing of the shaft by the vagina. Nothing. I looked down to make sure it was in. Yep, it was all the way in. Strange. Then I realized Barb had a very large vaginal tunnel, much bigger than I ever had imagined. It was like sticking my dick in a bowl of warm Jello. No feeling at all.

Out of habit, I started a thrusting motion, although I could not feel much. Evidentially this was normal for Barb, as she was making agreeable noises and even moving a bit. How odd. Maybe my dick shrunk again. I looked down again as I thrust in and out, it looked pretty normal. I needed some friction if I was going to come. I racked my brain and recalled in some smut novel I had read that the man put a pillow under the woman's ass to get a better angle and drill down deeper. That's what I'll do!

Barb was looking up at me and smiling while I was fucking her, which I thoroughly enjoyed. "Barb? I'm going to put a pillow under your hips. Raise up."

She got the idea, lifting up her ass while I put a pillow in place. During this, my dick popped out, so we went through the reentry procedure. I was soon fucking her at an angle, which was better but was not the feel I was looking for. She was really enjoying it.

"Oh, Dirk! This is fun! What a different feeling, I may have another orgasm!"

After another minute or so of deep thrusting, she gave another shudder and loud moan.

"Oh my! Oh! There! Another little orgasm. This is great!"

I did not have a lot of experience in observing orgasms, so I took her word for it and said, "I'm happy for you!"

Ready to try something else so I could come, I wittily said, "Want to try something else?"

She smiled again. "Sure! What do you want to do?"

I was ready for this one, my ex really liked it on top. "Let's put you on top, many women enjoy that feeling." I sounded so worldly.

"That sounds like fun, how does it work? I've never done it that way before."

Well, my dear, let old Dirk the sex expert show you. "I'll pull out and get on my back. Then you straddle my hips and raise up so my dick can get in you. Guide it in as you lower yourself down, as fast, or as slow as you want. When you are all the way down, start rocking your hips forward and back. You'll feel it right away if you are doing it right."

She grinned. "Okay! Here goes!"

I was wondering to myself as she moved into position, how could she not have done this before? Were sex positions like this not done in Indiana?

Barb got into position and with her hand on my now slimy cock, aligned the head with the correct hole and started to lower herself onto my shaft. As she did so, moans emanated from her mouth, even more as she was fully impaled on the now semi-rigid cock.

"Wow, that's in really deep!" she exclaimed. She began a motion that was more up and down instead of forward and back.

"That's good but you will really like pushing your hips forward into me." I put my hand in front of her pubic mound. "Just push forward with your hips, try and move my hand and try and rub your clit against my pelvis."

She tried the motion, and her eyes grew wide. "Oh, Dirk! That's great!"

I started pushing up into her as she ground her pelvis against mine. She was getting the idea. With my pumping up into her, her grinding the clit against me, and me taking some boob into my mouth and licking the nipple, she was getting quite excited. After a few minutes, she announced another orgasm.

"Oh! OH! I'm coming again! Oh, how nice! Arrrrrraaaahhhh! Wow!"

She was really good at verbalizing what she was experiencing. While glad she was having a good time, I needed to come in the worst way and was not even close. After enjoying some more with her on top, I was ready for some guaranteed ejaculation positions.

"Now I'm going to do you from behind. Climb off and get on your hands and knees."

"Okay! This is really fun, trying all these new positions!"

Again, I thought, what were the guys out here doing? Straight missionary position sex all the time? All the better for me to introduce this west coast stuff to the female population.

She assumed the position, and I moved in behind her. Her hand guided my cock to the correct hole, and I pushed in all the way. Still not a lot of feeling, but this was an almost guaranteed position for me to come in. I started pumping into her and she moaned as I did so.

"I've heard about this but had not tried it! This is really different!" She exclaimed.

I had been pumping her at about half speed. I reached down and grabbed one of her large boobs that was swaying back and forth, and played with the nipple while I fucked her. I needed to turn up the heat if I was going to come. I said, "I'm going to go faster and harder now. Let me know if it's too hard."

"Okay!"

I cranked up the heat and was soon going at her pussy hard and fast, with the sound of flesh against flesh slapping in the candlelight. Her boobs were flying back and forth, and the fat on her ass cheeks jiggled with each hard pounding. She was moaning loudly, not complaining but just making cries of pleasure. After a few minutes of this, I realized I was not going to come. Next position, please!

I stopped and while I caressed her ass and boobs asked her to get on her back again. She complied, and soon I was deep inside her again, pounding away like mad, trying to get my rocks off. I took her legs and lifted her ankles up onto my shoulders, leaned in, and pounded her exposed and vulnerable pussy hard. She was groaning hard, and I finally felt the pressure rising in my balls and knew that my orgasm was imminent. I gasped out, "I'm getting close, I'm about to come!"

She helped by gasping, "Come inside me, Dirk! Come now!"

I complied with her urging and shot a long, hot jet of cum deep inside her as I pounded her pussy and groaned loudly. I slowed and stopped as several small spasms shot forth, adding to the wet mess I had made of her cunt. I put her legs down and looked at her. She was smiling from ear to ear. "That was great, Dirk! You really made me feel good! I bet I had four or five small orgasms."

"I'm happy to be of service, Ma'am."

"Can I just ask you something?"

"Sure, Barb."

She looked unsure. "Did you do all that stuff with your wife?"

I smiled at her. "Yes, of course."

She shook her head. "If a man would do that to me all the time, I'd never let him get past the mailbox, let alone divorce him."

I laughed. "I'll do all that and more any time you want, as long as you don't try and put a ring on me!"

It was her turn to laugh. "Don't get worried, I'm not going to drag you to city hall just yet."

I was still inside Barb and there were fluids dripping out of her pussy, running down her crack to her asshole. Our laughing had made it worse. She had me reach for a bedside box of tissue and held a handful against her slit as I pulled out, then she got up and went to the bathroom to deal with the rest, holding the wad against her as she tried to walk without dripping. I took a handful of tissue and tried to swab myself off, thinking Dirk old boy, you can do this. You can face bachelor life alone and still get laid. It may not all be the best pussy in the world, but it's a hell of a lot better than jerking off.

Barb came back to bed, and we snuggled together, avoiding the wet spot that I had created. She lay against me with an arm across my chest, with one of her big, warm boobs up against me. She lifted it up and arranged it, so it lay across my rib cage. This was my first experience with big boobs, and I decided right then and there that I liked them. She then threw her big thigh across my legs and snuggled in, so we were in contact on our entire body length. I was quite comfortable. I put my arm around her back and helped her scooch closer yet.

She smiled up at me and gave me a quick kiss. I stroked her back and ass with the arm I had around her and could not resist caressing the boob that was in my line of sight. Her smile widened. "Do you like them? Do you think they are too big and floppy?"

I was enthusiastic in my response. "This is my first encounter with boobs of this size, and I must say I'm a fan! You can put them on my chest anytime. I'll warn you that if you do, I'm going to play with them!"

She giggled. "I hoped you would, that's why I put one up there for you to reach. Are you still horny? Want to go again?"

I thought for a minute. "I'm not ruling it out, I'm interested. Let's wait and see what happens. I've never done it one right after the other before."

She was still smiling. "You're showing me new things and I'll show you a few."

"That's fair. I've never heard of multiple small orgasms before. Have you always been that way?"

Her hand was playing with my modest chest hair, occasionally stroking my inner thighs. "Yes, I never have one big one all at once, although that one when I was on top of you was one of my biggest yet. I just get these feelings building up, then have a small orgasm, then go on to the next one, with several in one session. I would say I am very fortunate to do it that way. I hear there are some girls that never have even one orgasm, is that what you have found with all the girls I'm sure you have had?" she teased.

"I don't have all that much experience, so I can't say for sure, but some women just don't seem to have them. Or they do have them and don't let me know."

She looked puzzled. "So, the women that don't have orgasms, do they still enjoy sex?"

"They seem to, sometimes really asking for it, then just lay there and let me do them."

"Hmm. That's interesting. Poor things. Well, if they were capable of coming, I bet you could get them to."

I blushed. "Thank you, I guess."

She wasn't done. "No kidding, Dirk. You really know how to make a girl feel good."

"Thank you again. I felt great, too."

Her hips squirmed a bit against me, and her hand moved down to my cock. "All this talk of orgasms has made me a little horny again."

"I understand completely. What shall we do about that?"

She smiled. "Judging by the way your dick is reacting, I'd say we are going to do it again."

I was amazed at the way my dick was acting. It was getting stiff quickly, quite surprisingly so. I would have thought I needed a several-hour break to get hard again. The sexy talk, the boob rubbing, and her playing with my chest and thighs must have all contributed to the result.

My hands moved across her again, caressing every inch of her fleshy body as I explored her like I had never seen her before. Naked before me, she had her own beauty of self-confidence and sexual energy like I had never seen before. She was at home in her skin, and I was attracted to her on a very basic sexual level.

My caressing of her boobs and nipples increased, and she did something I had never even thought of. She lifted one boob toward my mouth, and pulled my head toward her, inviting me to kiss and nibble her nipple without a word being said. As I took the offered nipple into my mouth and gave the erect tissue a little bite, she moaned and her hips moved against my side, humping into me. This was pretty hot, and I could feel my boner getting stiffer. I was ready to mount her.

My hand went to her sopping wet pussy, slippery with the cum I had shot into her and her own love juices. I tickled the clit a little, getting a good moan in response, then pushed my finger into the hole, finger fucking her for a minute. She moaned deeply and shuddered a little. I wondered if that was orgasm number one. She gasped, "Oh yes! Yes!" so I figured I was right.

I rolled her onto her back, got between her legs, and placed the swollen purple head of my cock at the labia to see if she wanted to drive. She put her hand on my shaft and gently steered it into position. I gave an exploratory push and was past the labia and into her sloppy wet cunt in an instant. I shoved all the way in with my hips and got a reaction I'll treasure for the rest of my life.

"Oh, Dirk! It's even harder than before! Your dick is as hard as a rock!"

That's exactly the kind of thing a 25-year-old man likes to hear, so I started a heavy rhythm of stroking into her. There was just one problem.

With the added lubrication of a large dose of slippery cum I had shot into her earlier and normal vaginal lubrication due to being excited, Barb's big pussy had absolutely no friction. I couldn't feel anything except warm wetness. It was like my cock was waving around in a warm breeze. I'd need more than that to produce an orgasm on my end. In the meantime, she was enjoying it, so I kept up my hard thrusting to an accompaniment of moans and groans. She liked the hard dick, even though I could not feel it.

After a few minutes of hard pumping, she had a request. "Dirk, I want to get on top again!" I am all about everyone having a good time, so I pulled out and got on my back.

"Climb aboard!" I said, trying to be funny.

It worked, she giggled as she swung her big leg over me and swiftly inserted my dick into her. She went all the way down quickly, getting that hard dick deep into her pussy. A loud groan came from her as she started wiggling on my cock, getting her hips moving in the right direction. Her gratification was immediate. She moved her hips hard, back, and forth for a few minutes. Then her excitement reached a crescendo. "Oh! Oh! This is wonderful! Oh, my! Ahhhhhhh! I'm coming hard! Ohhhhhh!"

I kept up my end, thrusting up hard into her, even though I couldn't feel it. I had one of her boobs in my mouth and was squeezing the nipple of the other as she climaxed loudly.

"Ahhhhh! Oh, God! Oh my god! Ohhhhhh!"

Her pace slowed as the orgasm went through her, I could tell she was tired from her exertions. She slowed down to a slow rocking, her eyes closed and her lower lip between her teeth as her entire pussy tingled from the excitement. I pushed gently into her, making contact with the clit that I thought would like. She did. "Oh, that's nice. Please keep pushing for a minute more."

After a few minutes, she came back to reality, bent over, and smothered me with kisses. "Oh, Dirk! That was my best orgasm EVER! Thank you, thank you, thank you!"

"I'm so glad for you, Barb!"

Then a look of concern came to her face. "Did you come?" I shook my head. "Your dick is still hard, can you try?"

I told her I would do my best. "Let's put you on your back."

She readily climbed off, and with her on her back with her legs spread waiting to receive me, looked very sexy. The area around her crotch and thighs was a wet shiny mess from all the juices that were flowing. I intended to add to that mess in short order. I got into position, and she again took hold of my slimy shaft and placed it in position. I pushed straight in and started humping her hard. She moaned softly as I did so, enjoying the ride. There was no feeling at all. I tried lifting her legs up so I could get deeper, but while it was fun, I could tell I would not come. Then I had an idea.

I let her legs down and pushed her knees together. I then moved my legs outside hers. Now her legs were together, narrowing the vaginal opening and creating more friction. I could make more or less friction by moving my legs. I started thrusting again, this time to a very satisfactory feeling, more or less like a normal-sized pussy.

"How's that, Barb? You doing okay?"

She nodded assent. "That's fine. Does it feel good to you?"

It was what I had been waiting for. "Yes, it feels great!"

I ramped up my thrusting and was feeling it in my balls. She helped me out by saying, "Do it as hard as you want!"

I took the encouragement to heart and pounded away as hard as I could. She was moaning again, and as I shot my load of cum deep into her and groaned loudly with the release, she cried out again.

"Oh, that's good! Oh! Oh! Oh, my! I had another pretty good little orgasm!"

This was pretty amazing. I had never heard of multiple orgasms like this before, not that I had done any research into the subject. We did the cleanup routine again and lay back in the bed trying to avoid the multiple wet areas. She snuggled again into me, and this time as I caressed her back, noticed little rolls of flesh here and there. It was different and interesting, not repulsive at all, and I would learn later that was a characteristic of big women.

She had a direct question. "Did you put my legs together because I am too loose?"

Well, yes, but that would not be gentlemanly to say. "With the cum from our first session inside you it was still very slippery, and I wanted some more friction to help me come, so I narrowed the opening. It's just engineering at work." There, that was diplomatic. I may get invited back.

She giggled. "Sex engineering. I like that."

"I like that you have lots of orgasms. That's pretty wild."

"That last one was pretty good. I didn't expect that at all."

We lay there chatting while caressing each other in the candlelight, and I was starting to get very sleepy. She noticed and raised up.

"Dirk, I can't let you stay the night. If my son woke up while we were in bed together, I can't be sure he would not repeat that to the wrong people. Can I throw you out without making you mad?"

"Of course. Let me get dressed and I'll be on my way."

I found my clothes strewn around the makeshift bedroom. She turned on a light, which terminated the sexy ambiance. I got into my clothes, and she walked me to the door, wearing a robe cinched tightly around her. I took her into my arms and kissed her deeply. Her arms were around me tightly.

"Thanks for dinner and a lovely evening," I said politely.

She laughed. "It was indeed lovely. We'll have to do it again sometime. Will you call me?"

I kissed the end of her nose. "You can count on that."

BIG GIRLS NEED LOVE, TOO! BARBARA FROM KOKOMO 15

Outside in the frigid Indiana winter night, I walked carefully on the slippery sidewalk to my car, shivering with the sharp contrast between her warm house and the icy wind. As I waited for my defroster to make a dent in the light coating of frost, I smiled to myself. This bachelor stuff was not too bad. My outlook on life in general was improving.

Booty Call

After our initial date and great sex session, it was hard to get back together with Barb, even though we both wanted to badly. With my aircrew alert duty a week at a time taking a huge bite out of my schedule every three weeks, flying training missions, and doing Air Force ground training classes, we could not find a good day for another date. She was busy with her son's activities, seeing her Mother, and other life events. I got it.

Sometimes I stopped by her office on base to chat, but with her co-worker watching us closely and listening to our every word, it was awkward, especially since we both wanted to rip the other's clothes off. We talked on the phone every few days, and when I called her while she was alone at home, the conversations were steamy. Sometimes she would call me at the alert facility in the evenings when she was alone and had a glass of wine. The contents of those calls bordered on phone sex. It was great fun, but frustrating.

One frigidly cold night, my crew and I were debriefing from a great flight. Everything had gone well, we clicked together as a team, overcame some operational challenges, and felt at the top of our game. We had a few beers as we wound down from our night, and as the other crewmembers went home to their spouses, I felt the pangs of horniness emerging.

On a whim, I decided to call Barb at home, something I seldom did as her son would sometimes answer the phone, and while he knew who I was, I didn't want him telling his Grandma about the nice man that called his Mommy. Barb answered on the first ring, and I could visualize her sitting on the living room sofa. Hopefully, she had finished a glass of wine and was horny.

After a cordial greeting, I shyly stumbled on the reason I was calling.

"Well, Barb. I got done flying for the night, had a few beers, and was thinking about you ..."

She laughed. "Thinking about me, or thinking about asking to come over and have sex with me?"

She saw right through my fumbling attempt. "I'm not going to lie to you, I'd like to come over and ravish you."

She laughed again. "I'll turn the porch light on for you. Knock softly, my son is sleeping."

With that, I told her I would see her soon and possibly violated a few speed laws once I got off base, heading south to Kokomo. Pulling up to her small house, I tried to keep things quiet and knocked softly as she had requested. Answering the door in her robe, she looked like she was about to go to bed, even without me there. She had washed her face of makeup and her hair was a little disheveled. She still looked sexy, in a suburban mom kind of way.

She was smiling, which I was hoping for. "Come on in," she whispered, and I entered the foyer, and stopped to take my boots off. She laughed softly as she noticed I was still wearing my flight suit, jacket, hat, and boots. "Came straight from work without stopping to change? You must want it badly!"

I looked her straight in the eye. "You have no idea."

She smiled at me again, and said, "It's your lucky day. I want it, too."

I pulled her to me, and we had a nice, long deep kiss. She felt nice and warm under the robe. I had to ask, "Are you wearing anything under that robe?"

"Well, I was until you called," she said in a seductive voice. "You'll find out soon enough."

She led us to the couch. "I took the liberty of pouring us a glass of wine. Do you have time for that, or are you in a hurry?"

I smiled at her. "Now that I'm here seeing you like that, I have plenty of time." That got a chuckle out of her, and we clinked glasses.

We chatted a bit as we sipped the wine, talking about the trouble we had getting together. The TV was muted in the background, lending a comfortable ambiance to our rushed rendezvous. She decided to start talking about sex.

"What are you going to do to me tonight? Anything different? I learned a lot from our first encounter."

I had actually been giving that a lot of thought. "How about some oral sex, or maybe anal?"

She picked up on the subtleties of that. "Anal I'm not too sure about right now. Now oral, you've got my attention! You mean like a blow job for you or something for me?"

"I'm thinking of giving you a nice licking, you blowing me, then we can do it at the same time in a sixty-nine."

She grinned. "Oooo, that sounds like fun. I've done a little of both of those but not at the same time. The men that tried it on me treated me like I was an ice cream cone, licked it a little while, then wanted to get on me and hump me until they came. I hope there is more to it than that."

I smiled at her confidently. "I hope to make you scream with delight at the artistic way I will be licking your most intimate parts." I actually did not know too much about eating pussy but hoped it would all work out.

"Oh, my. I'm getting hot just hearing about that!" She opened her robe a little so I could see a boob. I appreciated the view, and so did my cock.

She smiled as she saw me taking in the view. "Would you like to unzip your flight suit and perhaps step out of it?"

"I'd like that very much." I stood, unzipped the Nomex flight suit, and carefully removed it, leaving me in my undershirt, undershorts, and dog tags. In response, she opened the robe a bit wider. I took off my undershirt.

She scooted closer to me and started to caress my chest and legs. I reached through the now wide-open gap in her robe and found a boob to fondle as we looked each other in the eye. We stayed in that state for a minute or so, then I leaned in and started kissing her. Her tongue hungrily responded, and our caressing became more wide-ranging. She slid next to me to make it easier to reach things, and after a while, we had full access to lots of warm skin. It was very enjoyable, and my dick was happy with the way things were progressing.

I bent down and took a nipple between my lips and brushed it with my tongue, causing her to moan with the pleasure it brought. She had found my dick and was tracing the outline of the rapidly swelling shaft through my underwear. I slid a hand down the robe and discovered she was naked underneath. There was a nice, warm patch of pussy and pubic hair under there between those big thighs, and my fingers went to the slit and rubbed the labia gently, getting a good moan out of her in response.

Barb then put her hand into my ever tighter underwear and wrapped her fingers around my dick and held it as she had before. She must like to feel it getting bigger. This time, it was fairly stiff, and she made a low approving sound deep in her throat. I slid the robe off her shoulders and enjoyed fondling her big boobs at the same time that I kissed her again. After a while of that, I decided to increase the heat.

"Barb, let me move the coffee table out of the way and I'll get my head between your legs."

She looked surprised. "Right here? On the sofa?"

I smiled at her. "Right here, right now. Keep your hips on the robe so we don't mess up the sofa."

She grinned in delight as I moved the furniture out of the way and knelt on the floor in front of her. I spread her legs wide and moved close to her pussy. I took a moment to admire the black pubic hair surrounding her lips and up her pelvis. I bent down and gave the labia a lick up and down to her exclamation of pleasure. The sights and smells

of the pussy were not unknown to me, and I took a secret pleasure in enjoying getting my face deep within and enjoying the aroma and texture of cunt.

I tried to not do anything resembling eating an ice cream cone, concentrating on spreading the labia and touching the pink interior with the tip of my tongue. On the way up to the top of the slit, I got a visual on the clitoris and gave it a light lick for fun. She moaned loudly when I did that, it must have been a hit. I went back down, this time with my tongue within the lips, licking from within. At the bottom of the slit was the hole leading to the vaginal vault. I did not know what else to do, so I stuck my tongue in there and gave it a wiggle. That turned out to be a big hit, as her hips squirmed madly, and loud moans escaped her mouth. I'd have to remember that spot.

Working my way back to the top, I recalled she liked the clit licked, so I gave it some love with gentle touches. For an added touch, I put my finger in the hole and finger fucked her a little while I licked the clit. She really liked that, as indicated by bucking hips and loud groaning. I kept that up for a while, then she groaned loudly and put her hands on the side of my head, running her fingers through my hair while crying out, "Oh, my. Oh! I'm going to come, Dirk! Keep it up! Oh! Oh! Don't stop!"

I kept up what I was doing as requested, and soon she shuddered and called out again.

"Ahhhhh! Ohhhh! Yesssss! Oh, that's so good! Mmmmmm! Oh, yes!"

She stopped shuddering and started talking. "Oh, Dirk! Oh my! How did you learn to do that? It was incredible! You've made me come by licking me, I would not have thought that was possible!" She was almost swooning. Her eyes had rolled back in her head, I thought she was going to faint. Good thing she did not know I was a pussy eating novice. I was pretty proud of myself. Time for the next act.

"Okay, time for you to return the favor. I'll sit on the couch and you get on your knees in front of me."

She had recovered enough to do just that, and I was soon receiving a very enthusiastic and sloppy blow job. I had to slow her down a little, maybe she was still worked up from the pussy eating. She was just bobbing straight up and down with her lips going up and down the shaft. I asked her to run her tongue around the shaft, and she did so. I could feel my cock stiffening with all the attention, and had to stop her before I exploded.

"Let's get on the bed now and do the sixty-nine." She rose up with a little saliva dripping from her mouth, which being the gentleman that I am, wiped off with my finger. She smiled and walked to the bed, totally naked. I could see her body clearly from behind, the first time I had done so, not counting when she was on all fours ahead of me in bed. Her thighs and ass were bigger than I thought, and I was amazed I had gotten so much pleasure from such a big girl. I definitely needed to change my way of thinking. I was sure there were a lot of big girls that wanted some dick, it had to be an underserved demographic. If the big girls of the world were anything like Barb, there was a lot of enthusiastic pussy out there waiting to be had.

She got on her back and looked at me with a big grin. She was excited to try new things. I really did not know which way was better, so I suggested we try both me on top and then her on top and see which was the most popular. I moved so I was face down on her pussy, carefully moved my legs over her head, and let her pull me down to the right altitude. She found the target and started in with a high-speed head job, while I buried my face in her wet snatch and found the slit and clit again. I repeated what worked last time, licking the clit and tonguing the hole. That was working well as there was a lot of moaning coming from the other end.

She was one of the most enthusiastic blow job artists I had run into thus far. What she lacked in skill, she made up for with verve. After a few minutes of this fun, I suggested swapping ends and we rearranged ourselves, with me maneuvering her large ass over my face until I had a good view of the target area. I pulled her down a little and was soon buried in wet pussy. It was wonderful. She went to work on my stiff rod and was bobbing her head up and down quickly, remembering to add the tongue around the shaft action every now and then. I slid my tongue into her hole and wiggled it again, which got a loud moan and hip wiggle in response. I worked my way back up her hairy crack until I got to her clit, and gave that a few licks. The level of moaning increased, so I figured I must be doing something right. After a few minutes of this, I was about ready to blow my load, so I called a halt to that and was thinking of what else to try when she asked to get on top. That sounded great to me, as she had a great orgasm while riding me.

I stayed on my back as she maneuvered her body over me, and after straddling me, took my slippery cock and lined it up. She slid down my pole to the bottom, with her face reflecting the great sensations she was getting from my cock being rammed all the way up in her. I again felt a nice warm sensation, but her pussy was so big, it really did not feel that great. She launched into rocking her hips back and forth, with me coaching her on the right angle. I had her big boobs swinging in my face and fondled one while I licked and kissed the other nipple.

I wet a finger in her plentiful pussy juice and explored her asshole by circling it. She looked at me with a raised eyebrow.

"Want to try just a finger?" I asked.

She nodded, so I gently slipped my finger in her ass and gave a few easy in and outs. Her eyes got big, and she moaned some more. After a minute I pulled it out and got back to pushing my rigid cock into her hard as she ground her pelvis against me like I taught her.

Soon she was moaning loudly and panting with the exertion. After about three minutes of being on top, she came loudly and hopefully did not wake her son up. I'd hate for him to describe what Mommy was doing to the nice man from the base.

"Oh, God, Oh, God, oh Dirk, that feels so fucking good! Damn! Ahhhhhhhhhh!"

Then she collapsed on me, breathing heavily and sweating between her boobs and on her face. "Whoo! That's a workout, but worth it! Wow!"

"I think you are liking being on top more and more!"

"You got that right! I'm so glad you taught me that. Oh, poor Dirk! You haven't come yet, have you?"

"Not yet. I'm going to put you on all fours and do it from behind."

She giggled. "I know you like that!"

Yes, I do, my big friend. "It's all about the excitement."

I got behind her and found she was sopping wet from my saliva and her pussy juices. This was going to be a waste of time unless something changed. I thought of something, just needed to present it diplomatically.

"Let me wipe you off a little, all that juicy stuff can't be comfortable for you."

She reached over and grabbed a strategically positioned cloth. "That's nice of you, I do feel pretty wet and sloppy down there."

I took the offered cloth and applied it everywhere there was moisture, even giving the labia a wipe. Things were much dryer, and I lined my cock up with the hole, and her hand was right there to guide it home. In I went, and it did feel better without all the wet stuff. I might even be able to come this way. I started a good rate of thrusting, and soon her big ass was jiggling, and her boobs were flopping back and forth every time I stuck it to her. The sound of slapping flesh filled the room, and I got hotter and hotter the harder I pounded her. I reached around and grabbed a boob and found the nipple to squeeze a little, then had to use both hands to hold on to her big waist to get in deep. Soon I was operating at maximum speed and intensity, and she hung on for dear life as I was pushing her all over the bed.

This felt great, but I wanted more. I pulled out and gasped, "Roll over. I'm going to drill you from the top." She rolled over quickly, her face flushed with excitement and anticipation of what was next. She spread her legs wide, which was very inviting. I moved up and was deep within her in seconds. I started a hard pumping, then lifted her legs high as she pushed up into me, groaning and moaning. I lifted her legs higher and moved her ankles apart until she was spreadeagled, her pussy exposed to my frantic pounding. She then surprised me by reaching around and putting a finger in my ass as she grinned. It was kind of interesting.

Harder and harder I pounded her, feeling the excitement rising in both of us. I was about to come in a big way. The finger in the ass was helping.

My balls erupted, and soon I was pumping a jet of cum deep within her as she moaned with excitement and hopefully not fear. I let go with a loud groan of my own and shared it with her as my breath came in gasps.

"Damn, Barb, that was a good one! How are you doing, I was riding you pretty hard."

She laughed, thank goodness. "I thought you were going to drive me right off the bed, then after you rolled me over, I've never been fucked so hard in my life! What a ride! I got excited by your enthusiasm and even had a little mini orgasm at the end! Wow! You'll have to call me after flying and a few beers more often if it's going to be like that!"

I love a satisfied customer. The drying off of all the excess moisture helped a lot, along with the fact that I was super horny. I was pretty pleased with how it all worked out.

"That was great, Barb. I'd hate to take advantage of your kind nature in letting me ravish you each time I fly."

"You let me worry about that, my friend. Are you going to let me up now?"

"Oh. Sure." I was still in her and holding her ankles up in the air. I caressed her as I backed out and got off her. She was a big, sticky mess between her legs and the cloth did all it could but could not take care of all the moisture I had added to an already wet pussy. She held the cloth between her legs and headed to the bathroom. I found some tissue in a box on the bedside table and swabbed myself off. My breathing was getting back to normal, and I lay back on the bed, pulling the sheet and blanket up over me. With the sweat drying on me, I was cooling off fast.

A pleasant second round

Barb rejoined me, and we engaged in some sticky snuggling. We kissed a little as we each tried to find a spot that wasn't covered in dried sweat or sticky residue. We needed a shower. It was getting late, and Barb had to get up for work and get her son off to school. I could feel her waiting until we both got enough snuggle time before she threw me out. I tried to beat her to the punch.

"When you are ready for me to leave, just say so. I don't want to keep you up too late."

She laughed. "Oh, are you one of those love them and leave them kind of guys? I was just trying to decide what to do next. I'm still real wet inside and pretty sticky, and just a little sore from that pounding you gave me."

"Oh, Barb. I'm sorry! I was too worked up."

"I'm not complaining, just stating a fact! That was one fun ride. No, what I was thinking is that you could go wash off your dick and then I would blow you until you came. You could even come in my mouth if you want. I don't mind and we damn sure don't need anything else sticky on this bed."

I could not believe my ears. "That's a hell of an offer, Barb. I'd love that!"

"The catch is I'm gonna make you help me change the sheets when we get done with that. They're a mess! Now, go wash up."

I went and made my junk fresh and clean, and returned to the bed. She was smiling, and immediately wrapped her hand around my cock as soon as I lay down next to her. She was keeping it nice and warm, which was appreciated. She wasn't done talking about blowing me.

"I figured if I make you come twice each time you see me, you'll keep returning for more."

"Aww, Barb. You don't need to do that. I'll come back and see you no matter what. We've just had trouble getting together."

"I know I'm not the prettiest girl in town, Dirk. I've got to keep you interested." She said somewhat bitterly.

I stroked her cheek. "You're a nice lady, Barb. I'm here, aren't I?"

"You want a blow job or not? Jeez." She let go of my cock with her hand and placed her mouth on it. I was not hard yet, and after a few minutes of rolling it around in her mouth, nothing was happening. "Too soon? We'll rest a while."

I went back to stroking her boobs, caressing her all over, and generally engaging in fun foreplay. She ran her hands over me as well and was kissing me heavily and was starting to get worked up again. I put a hand down to her pussy, and her hand stopped me.

"Dirk, it's really messy ..."

"You want to get fingered or not? Jeez!" I mimicked her previous comment.

"Yes, please. I just don't want you to get grossed out... Oh! That feels good!"

I ran my finger around her sopping wet pussy for a while and tickled her clit with each chance I got. She was moaning and squirming, and I figured the blow job was forgotten while I excited her. She then turned around to face the other way and got my dick in her mouth, giving me the opportunity to finger her and if I stretched, play with her boobs. That worked for me, and my cock woke up happy in someone's mouth and got nice and hard.

She was moaning and squirming, and another Barb orgasm was in the works. She blew me rapidly, with great effect, as her tongue rapidly and firmly swirled around the shaft and glans. She was really catching on for a blowjob rookie. After only a few minutes, I could feel the pressure building and called out the urgency of the situation.

I gasped out, "Barb! I'm about to come ..."

She moaned, groaned, squirmed, and sucked all at once. I kept up the sloppy fingering and boob play, and after a minute, I exploded in her mouth, which triggered her orgasm. We lay writhing into each other and as spasm after spasm of hot cum shot into her mouth, her body quivered, and she moaned loudly around a mouthful of sticky cock. After it was over, she raised her head and took a cloth that was next to us and spit the cum out into the cloth. She spit several times, and then wiped her mouth and lips, catching some stray dribbles that leaked out of the corner of her mouth. She stuck her tongue out and wiped that as well which was a good idea as it was coated with the stuff.

"Wow! That was a lot of cum. Looks like you didn't have sex for a year, let alone an hour ago!"

"What can I say, you get me worked up. That was great!"

She smiled shyly. "Did you really like it? I've never done it all the way in my mouth before."

"It may sound gross, but the evidence of how much I like it was in your mouth."

She laughed and got up. "I'm sorry, I have to go rinse this stuff out of my mouth. You can start stripping the bed."

I got up and started stripping the bed, which was a mess of rumpled sheets, wet spots, and general mayhem. It looked like someone had been fucking all night in it. She came back with her mouth rinsed out and we got the soiled stuff off and the new, fresh sheets on in no time. It's amazing how much faster it goes with two people.

I found most of my clothing and was zipping up my flight suit and reaching for my boots when she came to me and sat on my lap. She was a big girl, and I had to spread my legs a little to compensate for the load. She put her arms around my neck and laid her head against me.

"Dirk? Can we go on a real date sometime? So far, our dates have been here at the house having sex."

"Well, you did feed me lasagna once ..."

"You know what I mean. Can we go to dinner and a movie or something?"

"Sure. How about this weekend?"

She looked at me and smiled. "That would be nice. I'll get my Mom to watch my son. Saturday night?"

"Sounds good to me. I just have ground training on Friday, which will only take half the day, then I'm off until Monday."

She smiled more widely. "It's a date! Now get out of here and let me get some sleep, you sex maniac. It's the middle of the night!"

I kissed her goodbye and zipped my flight jacket up to my neck, reached into my leg pocket, got my flight gloves out, and put them on as I walked to the car. It was absolutely freezing. The wind cut through my jacket and flight suit like a knife. I shivered in the car driving back north until the heater started putting out warm air. When would winter end in this god-forsaken place?

Saturday

Barb and I talked a few times before we met on Saturday. The agreed-upon plan was for her to meet me at my trailer in the afternoon, then we would go to dinner in Peru and then catch a movie on the air base, returning to my trailer for an overnight visit. She had not been to my trailer yet, and I tried to prepare her for its general seediness. She didn't seem bothered by that, so I quit worrying about it.

Near the appointed time, she arrived and came into the trailer with a small overnight bag, which she sat down with a shy smile. It seemed as if she was nervous about spending the night. I took her heavy coat from her and kissed her and wrapped my arms around her, in a welcoming gesture, then I picked up her bag.

"I'll put this in the bedroom for you. Anything you want to hang up?"

She nodded. "I'll change before we go out." I wondered why she did not just wear those clothes now, but I never have pretended to understand feminine logic. I showed her through the small trailer, and in the bedroom, she opened her bag and hung a few things in my closet, got out some girl stuff, and looked around for the bathroom to set them down. I showed her the small bathroom, and she asked if she could look around. Shrugging, I said that was fine.

She came out of the bathroom with two washcloths, setting them on the small bedside table. With a shy grin, she said, "We may be needing these later." I did not comment on that.

We went to the kitchen, where I offered her something to drink, and to my surprise she picked wine. I poured us both some wine into my only suitable glasses, which were juice glasses. She took the wine and again asked if she could look around. I went to the living room and put on some music while she opened and closed all the cupboards and the refrigerator. Coming out to the living room to join me on the sofa, she shook her head. "You live like a bachelor."

I smiled and said, "There is a good reason for that."

"You need some more things. You can always go to the Goodwill store or the thrift shop on base. You don't need new things, just some more essentials. Knives, measuring cups and spoons, some cookware, a colander, stuff like that."

"That's a good idea. I lost a lot of that in my divorce and didn't realize it."

She wasn't done. "And your refrigerator. Looks like it is used for milk, eggs, and mixers for cocktails. Don't you eat vegetables or fruit?"

I got defensive. "I have, every now and then."

She shook her head resignedly.

We chatted for a while, sipping our wine. The noon weather had said there may be winter mixed precipitation this evening, so we talked about keeping an eye out for that. With no agenda in mind, I asked, "What time do you want to go to dinner and where?"

"If we go early, about 5:30, we should be back to the base in time for the movie."

"Sounds good."

"There is an okay family restaurant on Main, they have a little of everything."

"Also, good."

She smiled. "Which leads us to what shall we do between now and then, right?"

I could see where this was going. "A relevant query."

She blushed. "I was thinking you could look at my vagina and see if it's okay after you were rough with it a few days ago."

"I'd be glad to do that. Shall we go to the examining room?"

"As soon as I finish my wine." We did, and standing up, I took her hand to lead the way to the bedroom.

Afternoon delight

We arrived safely in the bedroom, and I started to unfasten her clothes. She had way too many on. I unbuttoned her blouse and removed it, with a short delay while she hung it up. "You need more hangers." I unfastened her bra, and her big boobs spilled out, causing me to divert my attention to their well-being by fondling them and bending down to kiss the nipples. She liked that, so I removed the bra and we spent a few minutes kissing while I played with the boobs and caressed her back.

She unbuttoned and removed my shirt and after another delay, while she hung it up, we faced each other nude from the waist up. She ran her hands all over my chest and back, with an approving "Mmmmm" sound from time to time as we kissed some more.

She pulled back and smiled at me. "I'm so glad you like kissing. Lots of men just want to grab my boobs, spread my legs, and go to town."

"I plan on doing all that. I think good kissing leads to good orgasms later."

She was still smiling. "You don't have any problems getting me to have an orgasm. Or four."

"Is four our record? I'll try and do better."

She laughed. "It's quality over quantity. Would you like to remove my pants? I'm getting pretty horny."

"I can do that!" I unfastened her slacks and slowly slid them down her legs, kissing her big thighs as I did so. She obligingly lifted each foot up in turn, and after neatly hanging them up, turned to me and started working on the belt and pants fastenings. After she slid my pants off and hung them up, we were naked except for our underwear. We embraced, ran our hands over each other, and explored the bare skin that was now exposed.

I led her to the bed, and we lay down on our sides, where she reached into my underwear and took hold of my very interested cock. With a smile, she said, "Mmmm. He's ready for action."

I rose up and slid her panties off, then kissed the clit and labia. "It looks fine to me," I said seriously.

She giggled. "Did you check the inside?"

"Oh, sorry. I'll do that now."

I slid a finger into her dripping wet pussy, straight into the hole. She was way turned on, gasping and moaning as I massaged her pussy from the inside. "Seems to be okay down here, too."

She gasped, "Oh, Dirk! Just get on me! I'm ready now!"

"As you wish, dear lady."

I shed my underwear and crouched between her legs as she spread them wide for me and put the head of my cock at the entrance to the vagina. She guided my rod into her, and since she was so loose and wet, I pushed in all the way to the hilt in one smooth thrust, drawing another gasp from her.

"Oh, it's so hard! I love it!"

These are great things for a 25-year-old to hear, and I went to work thrusting into her, to an accompaniment of groans and moans. She ran her hands all over my legs and back as I was working on her, and her hips pushed up at me in response. Before long, I heard a long moan, and then she announced her first orgasm.

"Oh, oh, oh! Mmmmmm! I'm coming! Ahhhh! Don't stop, get me another one!"

I kept up my thrusting and fondled her boobs as I did so. She pulled me down for a passionate kiss, then released me for more loud moaning. After a few minutes of nice thrusting, she made a request.

"Do it hard, like last time!"

I was all for that. The sexy position and doing it hard helped me come, the heat of it all compensating for her loose pussy. I lifted her legs and increased the rate, depth, and intensity. Her boobs and hair were flopping wildly as I pounded away.

"Harder, Dirk! Harder! Oh, please, harder!"

What's a guy to do? I spread her out and raised up, like I was drilling for oil, slamming into her pussy with each stroke. Her moaning and exclaiming were nonstop, and I felt an urge building in my balls as she came loudly.

"Yes! Yes! Oh, God! Yes! Ahhhhhh! Oh, God! Oh, it's wonderful!"

As she shuddered and moaned, I felt the pressure rising, I was about to explode. I gasped out, "I'm not going to come inside you this time!"

"Pull it out, Dirk! Put in on my belly!"

I pulled out, and within seconds, ejaculated my load onto her big stomach. She reached down and slowly pumped my slimy dick as spasm after spasm shot out, finally ending with some dribbles as we both panted. Smiling, she asked, "What was that about?"

"I wanted to keep your pussy nice for oral sex later. I just happened to think of it at the last minute."

"It was a good idea. I could have washed it out, but this is easier."

Then the damned phone rang. I had to let it go to the answering machine in case it was the Air Force calling. I sincerely hoped it was not one of my other girlfriends calling to invite me to play. Barb was listening intently, either for that scenario or out of curiosity. The phone and answering machine were out in the living room. I could hear a man's voice. Must be the Air Force. Whew.

As the answering machine recorded the message, I reached for a cloth and Barb and tried to clean up my mess. We got it wiped up enough that she could stand and go to the bathroom to wet the cloth down and do a good cleanup. I wiped my dick down with the other cloth and waited for my turn in the bathroom. Barb called out to me and with a grin offered to wash my now limp dick. You don't get an offer like that every day. With me standing close to the sink, she gently washed me off with warm water. It felt great. Drying off, I decided to see what the message was all about, so I pulled on my underwear and went out to the living room. Answering machines in those days recorded the message on a small cassette tape. I hit the button, and the machine started playing.

"Sergeant Caldwell, this is Lieutenant Colonel Martin from the squadron. Please return my call as soon as you get this message. I need a boom operator to fill in on alert ASAP." He gave his number and reiterated the importance.

My ethics said I should call him back right away, but I also knew I would get snagged for at least the entire weekend of alert duty. My name was at the top of the list alphabetically, and I had an idea that they called the single guys first so as not to have unhappy wives. Then I had a thought. I had consumed alcohol, and I could not assume duty for at least 12 hours. I was off the hook.

Barb came out of the bedroom with a towel around her, and I explained the situation. She was irate. "You mean they can call you and put you on duty, even though you had plans? That's awful!"

"That's the military for you. If they had wanted you to have a good time, they would have issued you one."

I decided to get dressed, then call the Colonel back, giving him time to find another poor soul to fill the need. The Colonel answered right away.

"Hello, Sergeant Caldwell. Are you able to assume alert duty?"

"No, sir. I had a glass of wine with lunch. I won't be legal until about 0100."

He sighed. "It seems many of the boom operators I have heard from have had alcohol today with lunch. I don't blame you, it's a day off for most. Thanks anyway. You're off the hook, enjoy the weekend. Look out for that winter precipitation tonight!"

With a clear conscience, I rang off and turned my attention to Barb, clad only in a towel while doing girly stuff and preparing to go out.

"Do you want some more wine, Barb?" I called out.

"Yes, please!"

I refilled her glass and took it to the bathroom, where I saw a variety of ladies' cosmetics spread out on my counter. I kissed her on the back of the neck. She smelled good, it was very enjoyable.

"Mmm. Thanks. This is the way to get ready to go out, just having had intercourse with a handsome man."

"I know of no more beautiful sight than a woman that has just had intercourse. With me of course!"

She laughed. "That's awful! Come back in a few minutes if you want help picking out clothes."

"Yes, Ma'am."

I went to the living room to watch the local weather. It was too early for an update, so I surfed the few channels available until Barb came out. She looked nice in a sweater and skirt outfit, with leggings for the cold. She was made up, with her hair brushed, sprayed, and jewelry on. She looked very nice, and I said so.

She did a turn in front of me, like a model. "Thanks, Mister Dirk. You make me feel pretty."

I went to her and kissed her. "You are pretty, don't let anyone tell you otherwise."

She put a hand on my cheek and gazed into my eyes. "You're a nice man, Dirk."

After a minute, I said, "We should go eat before we fall back into bed."

Date Night

She decided the clothes I had on were suitable for Peru, Indiana nightlife and we went out into the cold wind. We found a nice place in town called Froggy's and enjoyed a drink and dinner. It was fun and we chatted about many things that we had not had time for before. I was getting to know her and decided she was a nice lady. I began to hear warning bells that she wanted a Daddy for her son, but it was not obvious. We were two people that had an attraction and turned each other on in bed but could also be friends.

We finished dinner and went back out into the cold, wet wind. I was keeping an eye on the weather, and it was dicey but okay. We went to the air base and sat down for a movie starring an unknown actor named Billy Crystal. It was a funny movie, and we held hands for much of it, feeling much like an established couple. I saw a few Air Force folks I knew in the lobby, introduced them to Barb, and we all chatted. After the movie, we went out into the start of freezing rain and sleet, and I was glad to pull my car up to the trailer and dash inside, slipping and sliding on the slick wooden porch.

Standing inside the trailer, dripping, I took our coats and hung them on the back of chairs in the kitchen. I made us each a cocktail of vodka and orange juice, and we sat on the sofa to chat. I kissed her, and she smiled at me.

"That was fun, Dirk. It felt like a real date."

"It was a real date. Dinner and a movie, an American classic."

"I mean, when you came to my house the other night, I thought you only wanted to use me for sex."

She was right, but I had to think of a diplomatic way to say it. "We had been trying to see each other, and the thought of seeing you on the spur of the moment was exciting."

Laughing, she said, "You are a smooth talker. It's all right, just remember a girl likes to be dated along with the sex. Tonight more than made up for it, but I have a question for you. Was it awkward to introduce me to your friends at the theater on base?"

I was puzzled. "Why would that be, Barb?"

"Well, their wives were all young, pretty, and … thin. I'm not any of those. I'm older than you, and it seemed like I did not fit in."

I took her hands in mine. "Barb, you are a pretty lady. I'm not worried about your age or anything else. Besides, if any of those guys knew how freaking hot you are in bed, they would be climbing over me to date you. It's my secret. I'm not sharing you with anyone."

She put her drink down, then flung her arms around my neck. "Smooth talker! You know just the right things to say to an insecure female." She gave me a big kiss and looked into my eyes from six inches away. "You may get lucky tonight."

"One can only hope but being with you is reward enough."

She laughed as she let go of my neck. "Oh, Sergeant, you are so full of it."

The mood lightened, and we continued chatting and sharing our life stories. She had been in the area her entire life, had been married, and had one kid. She liked working at the base education office for the civil service benefits but was thinking of finding a higher-paying job. I sensed she was looking for security, and I was wondering if she was going to include me in that vision. I had made my statement when we first met that I was unequivocally not looking for a long-term relationship, leaving no room for doubt. I wondered if she really had been listening to that part. Sometimes good sex creates tunnel vision, and she was enjoying the sex.

We finished our drink, and I asked if she would like another. It's not like I needed to get her drunk to remove her inhibitions.

"Yes, please. I'll be right back."

I went and made two more of the simple drinks and made myself comfortable on the sofa. She returned after several minutes, having changed outfits. Barb was now wearing a long, white, very translucent nightgown. It had a jacket, lacy bra, and string panties that were pretty skimpy. I could see her nipples and pubic hair faintly through the thin material. She had brushed her hair, reapplied lipstick, put different jewelry on, and I could detect the scent of nice perfume. She looked great.

"Barb, you look fantastic!"

With a big smile on her face, she did a model turn in front of me, then sat down next to me.

"Thank you. I wanted to look nice for you on our first real date night, so I picked this up. I'm glad you like it."

"I do indeed, I'm just not sure how long you will have it on."

She laughed. "I'm sure it will have the desired effect soon enough, then find its way to the floor."

My cock was stirring already. "I'm feeling the effects already."

She reached over and felt my crotch for a moment. "Mmmm. Getting a reaction, I see. Let's work on our drinks."

We sipped our cocktails and continued chatting as if there was not a hot, scantily clad woman priming the sex mood. I admired her, trying not to make her self-conscious.

"Do you mind me looking at you?" I asked.

She smiled shyly, "I guess that's why I'm wearing it. Now it seems like you are overdressed."

"You could do something about that."

She leaned over and unbuttoned my shirt and spread it a little. "Good, now I can see your chest hair."

In return, I leaned over to her and moved her jacket to see her boobs better, the darkness of the nipples and areola showing provocatively through the thin material.

We sat like that for a minute, then she reached over to unfasten my belt buckle and my pants, opening them a little. Smiling, she said, "I can see the outline of your dick now, kind of pushing at the underwear like it wants out."

"It likes you looking at it."

We each took another sip of our drink and took in the other's visual treats. I could not stand it anymore and moved one of the flimsy bra cups over, so I could see the erect nipple. It was a nice sight.

It was her turn, and after a while, she slid my shirt down off my shoulders. My bare chest was available for her to admire, and she did.

I then decided to increase the heat. "Can you turn your knees towards me and spread your legs a little so I can see your bush?"

That made her grin as she did so and upped the ante by running a finger along the edge of the panties and sliding them over a bit so I could see the hair and slit. Now I could see a little of the labia showing, and she ran her fingers along the edge of the lips. A small moan escaped her mouth, surprising her.

All I could say, was, "Wow."

She was looking at my cock, still hidden by underwear. I helped that along by pushing my underwear down enough for my dick to be freed. He liked the open air, standing up and bobbing a bit.

I said, "Put a finger in." She knew what I meant, and slid her index finger into her pussy, moaning again. Her face showed her excitement, and her eyes were half closed. Without me asking, she worked it up and down, rubbing her own clit, then going back in, all the way to the knuckle.

I took my cock in hand and pumped it a little since she was keeping herself busy. After a minute, I stopped that and picked up my drink, and took a swallow. She pulled her finger out, and took a drink, too. We smiled seductively at each other, enjoying the foreplay. Outside, the frigid wind howled, and we could hear sleet hitting the sides of the trailer. The trailer had a good heater, and we were warm while playing our games.

She set the glass down and resumed her fingering action, adding to it by fondling her own nipple and boob, moaning as she did so. I stroked my rock-hard dick and watched her. It was pretty damned exciting. After a minute she pulled the finger out to move it elsewhere, and I reached for her hand and took the index finger, wet with pussy juice, into my mouth and sucked it clean while rolling my tongue around it. Her eyes rolled back in her head, and a loud moan came from her mouth as she shuddered, then her eyes focused and she smiled at me in satisfaction. "That's the first one. I'm sure there will be more."

I invited her to sit on my lap, and she did so at a ninety-degree angle. I ran my hand between her legs and stroked her labia through the now-damp panties. I kissed her passionately, and her hand sought out my rigid cock protruding up from my lowered pants. During the kiss, I slid my finger into her pussy, going right for the hole of the vaginal vault. She moaned in her throat while I had my tongue in her mouth, turned on mightily.

We were going to come right here on the couch, so I pulled my hand back and handed her drink to her and took a swallow of mine. We both drank for a minute, then setting the empty glasses down, went back to work. This time, I caressed her boobs, while she played with my hair and rubbed the back of my neck while nibbling my ear lobe. I found her pussy again, and went up and down the slit, paying particular attention to the clit. She groaned appreciatively and went back to my cock with her fist closed around it. She always just held the cock, not pumping it. Interesting. If she had pumped it, it would have gone off, so it was all working out.

Things get Hot

We stayed engaged like that for a while, ignoring the wind and sleet, while we worked each other up to a frenzy of lust. She had a plan.

"Do me from behind again, then I'll get on top!" she gasped out.

"Here or in the bed?"

"Mmmm. A little of both."

She slid off my lap onto the sofa, and I stood up and divested myself of any remaining clothing. I took her hand and led Barb to the small recliner chair that I had gotten in the divorce, and bent her over it, with her facing into the chair, holding the armrests. I untied the small bows holding the panties on and tossed them aside. I moved behind her and slid my cock all the way to the hilt without stopping, getting a warm sensation from her dripping wet, loose pussy but that was about it. She needed a drying off, but that would have to wait.

Holding her big waist, I started a powerful thrusting motion and watched her butt jiggle and boobs bounce each time I pounded in, hearing the slapping of flesh on flesh. She moaned excitedly and kept raising her head and tossing it around, becoming overwhelmed with excitement. Then she said the darndest thing.

"Slap my ass, Dirk! Spank me on the ass!"

I did not know what to think, so I popped her on one of her ass cheeks.

"Harder! Spank me harder!"

Well, hell. It was her idea. I slapped her ass harder and heard an audible pop as I did so.

"Again! Harder!"

I spanked her a few more hard ones and was rewarded with a very loud exclamation.

"Ahhhhhhh! Oh, shit! Oh, God! Arrrrrrrr! Ohhhhh! Shit! I'm coming! Rub my clit! Oh, please rub my clit!"

I did as she requested and felt her shudder from her head to her toes.

"Damn! That was a good one! Shit! Ohhhhhh! Pull out!"

I did as she requested, and she spun around, dropped to her knees and took my dick into her mouth, starting a rapid blow job. I was confused, yet happy. After a minute, she gasped out, "Bedroom!" and I got the idea.

We got up, and I took her hand and led her to the bed. I got on my back, and she climbed up immediately and mounted me, taking me all the way in with one push of her hips, groaning loudly.

She started her favorite hip-thrusting movement, and I rammed up into her as hard as I could. After a few minutes of that, she whispered loudly. "I want you to spank my ass again."

"Okay."

I slapped her ass a few times, and she moaned loudly, and a few seconds later started screaming softly.

"Ahhh! Keep spanking me! Harder! Oh, god, oh god, oh god, oh shit! Harder, Dirk! Ohhhh! I'm coming again! Oh, damn!"

Her big body quivered all over with reaction, and she collapsed on top of me, with me still pumping into her frantically. I of course stopped spanking her, and she lay with her chest heaving in great gasps on top of me as I kept pushing into her, desperately trying to come.

She sat up after a minute, and gasped, "Do you want to fuck me in the ass now?"

That got my attention.

"Are you sure?"

"Yeah, I know you have been wanting to do it. After you put your finger in my butt last week, I was wondering what your dick would feel like in there. I'm feeling kinky tonight, so go ahead."

Surprised, I said that would be a great idea, and she got on all fours, and bent over while I applied Vaseline from my bedside table to her anus and my dick, while she still breathed heavily. I used a cloth and gave her pussy a quick wipe to get all the excess juice cleaned up, then eased my cock to her asshole and pushed gently, feeling the sphincter stretch while she gasped. Pushing in slowly, the anal ring slowly yielded to the large purple head of my cock, and with a slow shove I was in her ass.

She groaned, "Oh, man! Why did I ask you to do this! It hurts!"

I stopped.

"Want me to pull out?"

She shook her head.

"No, it's getting better. Keep going. Fuck my ass, damn it!"

Pumping her slowly, she moaned and groaned. The tightness of her ass was fantastic after the sloppy wet pussy. I reached around and gave her clit some attention, and soon she was moaning nonstop as I stroked in and out of her ass. In a minute, she screamed softly and her whole body shook as she came again.

She gasped, "Harder! You can do it harder!"

With that invitation I pushed a little harder and faster, admiring the view of my cock between her big ass cheeks going in and out of her asshole. I didn't want to take advantage of her and do it too hard, and I was ready to come anyway.

Groaning loudly, I exploded deep within her in a long, fantastic orgasm and nearly collapsed myself. I lay on top of her back as she waited patiently, then I eased my cock out with a plop and admired the cum leaking out of her asshole. I rolled off her after a minute, and she put the cloth between her butt cheeks to catch the cum dripping from her ass and then rolled over and moved to lay against me. She looked into my eyes from a foot away, grinning.

"Damn. Dirk. That was pretty hot!"

"No shit. Why did you want me to spank you, then do you in the ass?"

She looked sheepish. "I read about that in one of those erotic novels and wanted to try it. If I'm going to try anything new, it's gonna be with you. Did you like it?"

"The spanking was a turn on, but I've never done that before. Did it turn you on?"

"Yeah, the pain made me come quicker, and that's when I decided to let you do anal. I know you've been wanting to. I don't think I'll have you do that all the time. Just special occasions."

"Like date night?"

She laughed. "On some date nights, maybe. Or your birthday."

I raised up. "Let me see your butt."

She had several red marks, all on the fleshy part of the ass. "You may get some bruising. I don't want to get arrested for domestic violence."

"I don't think that's applicable when I asked for it."

I stroked her cheek. "That was some intense stuff."

She smiled. "Yes, it was, in a good way. Does vodka make you lose inhibitions?"

I laughed. "Probably. That was fun sitting there drinking and doing visual foreplay."

"Yes, it was. How do you think of these things?"

Smiling, I said, "I must be reading those same novels you are."

We each took a trip to the bathroom to clean up our sticky parts and I washed my dick thoroughly, then came back to bed. She had found all the parts of her nightgown and put them back on. I admired how that looked and told her.

She smiled but said, "Down, boy! This girl has to rest before starting another episode." She rubbed her butt a little. "My butt cheeks are going to ache tomorrow, and my butt hole is sore already."

"If you show up with a whip for our next date, be advised I am not doing that."

"Agreed! Is it too early to go to bed?"

I looked at the clock. "We could have a nightcap and watch the 11:00 o'clock news if you want."

"That sounds nice. Do you have a small blanket we can cuddle up with together on the sofa?"

"No, but I have a thin regular-sized blanket in the closet, I'll get that."

"Add a small cuddling blanket to your shopping list, Dirk."

"Yes, Ma'am."

We curled up together on the sofa under the blanket with a drink and watched the news and the weather. The sleet had stopped, and bitterly cold weather was on the way for Sunday. After the news, we sleepily went off to bed and snuggled a little before going to sleep.

Sunday Morning Regrets

We had a good night's sleep, and she was dressed, packed, and ready to depart soon after rising. The coffee was still brewing when she was ready to leave. We kissed briefly, then I went out and started her car to get the accumulation of ice off the windows. It was colder than hell outside, probably in the teens, and there was residual ice everywhere.

"This is going to take a few minutes, Barb. Might as well have some coffee."

She seemed pretty unsettled this morning. In reality, it was our first morning together.

"Is everything okay, Barb? What's wrong?"

"I don't know! I'm just nervous this morning. Maybe it's being here overnight, I'm not sure I was ready for that. It feels so ... sudden."

I took her in my arms and held her, stroking her hair. I did not know what to say. Her arms went around me, but I could not comfort her. I finally got enough ice cleared from her windows for her to drive safely, and she left with a wan smile. Puzzled, I went back inside for coffee and to warm up. Overnight nerves? Regret from a kinky sex episode with spanking? I had no clue.

On Monday, I called her at her office to see if she wanted to meet for lunch, or a drink after work to talk. She was evasive, then agreed to a quick drink at the NCO Club on base after work. Still nervous, we got a drink and looked for a quiet table to be able to talk. Once seated, I asked her to tell me what was wrong, why she was so upset Sunday morning and nervous now.

"I just don't know, Dirk! I think waking up next to you on Sunday made me think things were moving too fast in our relationship."

I was baffled. Moving too fast? We had been together three times and had one overnight date.

"Barb, I'm not sure I understand. You wanted to go on a date, and we did. Did you not want to spend the night, is that what you mean?"

"Oh, I just don't know. I'm all confused about us."

Us? Oh, boy. I could see where this was headed. I needed to put a stop to this right now.

I took her hand and said gently, "Barb, I told you when we first met that I am not looking for any kind of relationship, long-term or otherwise. Did you think our dating and staying overnight is heading toward a commitment of some kind? Because that is not where I am headed."

She nodded her head, and sniffled a little, on the verge of tears.

"Honey, we're dating and having fun and sex right now, that's all. Don't confuse lust for love. I've been down that road before, and it ain't pretty when the lust runs out."

"But Dirk, it felt like we were more serious, with the kissing, the hugging, cuddling, and the sex. Are you feeling serious?"

"No, Barb. I love being romantic with you, playing boyfriend and girlfriend, but that is to make it more fun for both of us. I'm not going to get serious. Are you?"

She shook her head and blew her nose.

I said, "Okay, then. Let's see one another when the time is right and take it from there. If you want to date and not be romantic, I'll adjust to that. If you don't want to see me again, I understand."

"No, Dirk. I want to see you again. Give me a few days to get my emotions under control."

I kissed her hand. She got up to leave, and I walked her to the door. After she left, I went into the bar area and found some of my squadron mates and joined them.

One of my friends said, "Hey Dirk, how's that lady I saw you walk out the door with?"

I could only shake my head. "Women. I love them, but they drive me crazy."

"Amen! I'll drink to that!"

Let's try another date

On Wednesday, Barb called me after work and said she was ready to try another date. We checked our calendars and decided that Saturday was a good day and made some tentative plans. She did not want me to stay overnight at her place, so we agreed on the same scenario as the previous week. She would meet me at the trailer, we would venture out for dinner and either a movie or go somewhere else. As I hung up the phone, I sincerely hoped the morning after would go smoother.

I mission planned on Thursday and flew early on Friday. It was a short flight, air refueling a B-52 bomber and right back to the base, my favorite profile. As we walked into the squadron carrying all our flight gear, I heard a voice call out my name as we walked by the operations officer's office. Uh oh, what did I do now?

"Sergeant Caldwell! Come in here, please."

I dropped my gear in the hallway and turned back for the office, with my crew all making faces as if I were in trouble and was called into the Principal's office. My Chief was in the office as well, and he and the ops officer were staring at the schedule board posted on the wall.

The Chief said, "Pick up your flight gear and hightail it out to the alert facility. Sergeant Yarbrough's wife was not expected to go into labor until next month, but she's having contractions and abdominal pain now and may be in early labor. Jim is on alert and needs to be relieved right now so he can take her to the hospital. I'll try and get someone to relieve you as soon as I can, but you need to get out there pronto! Get moving!"

In the military, there is only one answer. "Yes, sir." I grabbed my gear and looked down the hall where my crew had gone to debrief. The Chief said, "After you assume alert duty, you can come back here and finish up the paperwork. Move!"

I moved. I pulled up to the alert facility parking lot and saw Jim and his pilot waiting for me. Jim was trying to start his truck, but with the bitter cold, it would not turn over. I told him to take mine and go take care of his wife, and we would figure it out later. I pulled the keys off my key ring and handed them over. Jim jumped in my car and left in a cloud of dust and gravel, and I was left behind looking at his pilot, Major Van.

"Hello, Dirk. Thanks for coming out so quickly. Jim is really worried."

"Hello, sir. Should we take my gear out to the plane? The Chief said he and the ops officer would try and get me relieved soon, and I need to be off this weekend. I have a date and don't want to miss that."

We agreed that a trip to the squadron was needed, so with my gear in the truck, we headed back to consult with the operations staff. Major Van asked me to let him work on getting a replacement, so I found my crew that I had just flown with sitting in the debriefing room, filling out paperwork and drinking a post-mission beer.

"So sorry you can't have a beer with us, Dirk!" the navigator said, laughing.

I decided to hold my tongue and stay out of trouble but extended my middle finger in his general direction in a show of discourtesy. I finished the paperwork, said goodbye to my crew, and went back to the ops office. I found that there were now three people staring at the schedule board, all looking frustrated.

The ops officer was the first to speak. "Caldwell, I'm going to have to keep you on alert with Van until Monday. We have no EC-135 boom operators available until then, you're it."

I tried to get sympathy. "But Colonel, I have a big date this weekend, and ..."

He held up his hand. "That's all, Sergeant."

Major Van and I left the office with the Chief. I verbalized that I had no clothes, no personal effects, or toiletries with me and was stuck on base.

The Chief was sympathetic. "See if you can get your crew to run out to your house and get your things, since you're on alert and can't leave the base. If they can't do it, let me know and I'll go out there myself after duty hours." That was kind of him. I hurried to find my crew, but they had vanished, knowing better than to hang out at the squadron on a Friday. Damn it anyways.

Major Van said we had better go get me on the access roster for the plane and put my gear onboard to be legal. We did that, and afterward, I tried calling my crew, to no avail. Then I called some of my friends, and that did not work either. I was resigned to going back to the squadron and giving the Chief my trailer keys. Driving back to the squadron, I was passing by the education office where Barb worked and thought I had better tell her of the change in plans in person rather than on the phone.

I entered her office. Barb was on the phone, and her nosey co-worker was not, asking if she could help me. I was pretty sure she knew Barb and I were dating, so I said I would wait for Barb, and sat down in the waiting area. After a few minutes, Barb came out with a smile. "What a surprise! What are you doing here?"

I asked if we could talk privately, and we found a small counseling room and went in there. I gave her the bad news. As expected, she was mad about the cancellation and ranted for a couple of minutes about how Air Force people could not plan their lives at all without something coming up to ruin things. She was not wrong. When she calmed down, she said, "Tell me again about your Chief having to go to your trailer and pack you a bag." I did, and she shook her head.

"Dirk, I'll go out there after work and get your things. Your place is close by, and I already have an idea where your stuff is. Tell the Chief it's taken care of."

"Aw, Barb. You don't have to do that."

"No, Dirk. If I'm going to be involved with an Air Force guy, things like this will happen. I've got to learn to deal with it. It's really no problem."

I thanked her profusely and after giving her a list of the items I needed, we arranged to meet at the squadron about 1700. I went to hand her my key ring. She stopped me.

"Give that to me in front of that old biddy I work with after I ask for them. Just follow my lead."

We went back to the office, and I said goodbye to both of the ladies, when Barb said innocently, "Oh! Dirk, I'll need your house keys. I'll see you later." I handed them over, looked at the co-worker whose mouth was hanging open, and left. Women.

With time to kill, I went back to the alert facility. Major Van was waiting for me at the desk. After hearing about my busted plans for the weekend, he offered, "We are having a crew dinner at the visitation center tomorrow afternoon, then the entire crew and their families are going to the base theater to catch the movie afterward. Why don't you come, and invite your girl to join us? I talked to my wife already, and we feel bad that you had to ruin your weekend to cover for our boom operator."

The visitation center was a recreation building just for alert crews, with a living room and kitchen setup, some small rooms to visit in, and some stuff for little kids to play on. It and the theater were a few of the places we could go while on alert. I thanked the Major for his offer and said I would check with my girlfriend.

He added, "If she comes and wants to bring something, make it a dessert. That's what Diane was going to bring if she had not gone to the hospital."

I was back at the squadron at the appointed time, met Barb, and extended the invite to her.

She shrugged. "I might as well come; I need something to do anyway. My Mom already had plans for my son, so I would be at home by myself tomorrow. I picked up the laundry from your trailer, you have several loads. Were you planning on doing the wash today before entertaining me tomorrow?"

I looked sheepish. "Ahh ..."

She laughed. "That's what I thought. Bachelors! I'll do it tonight at my house and drop it off before I meet you tomorrow. Where do I meet you?"

The visitation center was just across the street from the squadron. "You can park here; I'll watch out for you."

I got my suitcase out of her car and put it in the truck. We looked at each other for a minute. I broke the ice. "Would you like a kiss goodbye?"

She smiled. "A kiss with no obligation? What do we call what we are doing, Dirk?"

"Friends that are romantic when they are together but without a long-term commitment? I don't honestly know what to call it."

Leaning over to be kissed, she put her arms around me. I did a thorough job.

She smiled. "Mmmm. That was nice. See you tomorrow. We'll have to figure out what to call this."

I sincerely hoped she would not get upset and attach feelings of love to sex and romantic behavior. I headed back to the alert facility to keep the Soviet Union at bay and keep the world safe from communism while wondering what the chow hall was serving tonight.

A new meaning of Visitation

The next afternoon, I went to the visitation center with my borrowed crew in two vehicles, as I thought Barb would not care for the movie and I did not want to get stuck having to ride with the rest of the crew. The other crew member's families showed up at about the same time, and the visitation or "viz" center was a cacophony of happy kids playing and spouses getting ready to arrange the meal. Barb showed up on time, and after introducing her around, we found a couch in the corner that was isolated enough that we could carry on a conversation in private while still appearing to be participants. She had offered to assist the spouses and was excused from meal prep duty, as it was all under control.

As we sat in our corner, I gave Barb a quick kiss to let her know I was still interested and settled in to talk about relationships. We held hands as we sat, the epitome of a cute couple dating.

She asked, "Dirk, isn't there something about public display of affection while in uniform? Can you get in trouble?"

"Yep, PDA. In the viz center, that is suspended by informal understanding so families can relate normally. In theory, kissing you in the parking lot would be a no-no but guys do it all the time. I feel comfortable holding your hand and giving you an affectionate kiss. Prolonged deep kissing and breast fondling would be frowned upon."

"The military has a lot of rules."

I laughed. "Yes, they do."

After a while, all the adults sat at a long table and ate, while the kids were elsewhere. Major Van's wife did a good job of including Barb and me in the conversation and made us feel part of the crew. I had a good time, and it seemed Barb did as well. Afterward, we all helped clean up the mess, and it was decided when to leave for the movie. Barb and I opted not to go to the movie with the crew, and Major Van arranged the transportation so I would have a vehicle while they all went to the theatre. Other crews had come in with their spouses and kids, so there was a mix of men wearing flight suits, wives and girlfriends in pretty outfits, and kids being kids. We went back to our couch with the dessert that Barb had supplied, and after, watched the TV while holding hands. It was very comfortable.

We were fairly secluded from prying eyes in our corner, and after a while, Barb put her hand on the inside of my thigh, which I enjoyed. Then she ran her hand down my left leg, and when she came into contact with the inner thigh pocket where I had stowed my official US Air Force MC-1 hook-bladed survival knife, she looked up at me in surprise and astonishment. To her, it seemed like I had an enormous erection, when in fact it was my aircrew knife in the specified pocket according to regulation. I chuckled, and in a low voice assured her that the action was higher up on my leg.

She was pretty happy playing with my legs while that action was out of view from the rest of the room. I was responding to that with a swelling cock, when my rental crew all left for the movie, leaving me and Barb alone in the corner with just a few people remaining in the center. She leaned over and whispered in my ear, "Dirk? I'm getting really horny. Is there somewhere we can go?"

Now, normally there are few words a 25-year-old Air Force crewman would want to hear more than what Barb had whispered in my ear. The trouble was, while there was motive and desire, there was little opportunity for fulfillment. I wasn't sure if she was serious or just playing an extended foreplay game until I could get off alert. I whispered back, "There's nowhere to go except for outside or my squadron."

She smiled as she rubbed my crotch. "Let's go to the squadron."

We walked out into the freezing night with as much dignity as one can muster with a raging hard-on protruding from one's flight suit and walked across the street hand in hand to the darkened building that was my squadron. I used my key to unlock the side door, and we entered quietly and surmised we were alone. I thought of a small couch in the Chief's office, but quickly realized it was too small. I headed for one of the three small mission planning rooms with Barb in tow, entered, and shut the door. We were as alone as we could be under the circumstances.

We embraced, and Barb was now the aggressor, kissing me deeply and running her hand up and down my groin. She reached up and unzipped my flight suit down to the crotch and reached into my bulging underwear. I asked her, "What do you have in mind?" about the time her hand found my now exposed cock.

She whispered, "I want you to fuck me right here."

Now, those were words that surpassed the previous announcement. Not quite understanding how it would all work, I worked my hand into her slacks, and going deep, found some damp pubic hair under her panties. I took off my flight jacket and laid it on the grey metal and plastic mission planning table, and together we hoisted her ass up onto the jacket, protecting her bare bottom from the cold, impersonal government table. She pushed her slacks and panties down to her ankles, exposing knee-high nylon stockings that I decided were doing no harm, so I left them in place. I looked down at her as she spread her legs as much as she could with the constraints of the slacks and panties, while she pulled me to her by the cock.

I put a finger deep into her pussy, and she moaned softly. She was wet and ready for action. She had pulled my cock to the lips of her labia, and with a shove of my hips toward her, and hers toward me, I was in her. I pushed in, and soon was feeling the familiar warm and wet feeling without a lot of friction. The heat of the moment soon overwhelmed the lack of feeling from her loose pussy and I started a rapid, powerful thrusting as she pulled me deeper into her with both hands on my ass, groaning madly. We thrashed together as I fumbled for her boobs, sliding my hand under her sweater to find that soft, warm flesh. I was banging her so hard the table rocked back and forth, and for a moment I wondered what the weight capacity was.

We moaned and groaned together, her ass sliding around on the orange nylon of my flight jacket. She pulled me into her, and gasped, "Harder! Harder, Dirk! Oh, please fuck me harder!"

With that encouragement, I pushed into her as hard as I could, given the circumstances. I was pounding into her hard, and after a minute, her breathing became rapid and ragged, and she called out loudly, "Oh! Oh, God! Ahhhhhhh! Oh, god Dirk! I'm coming hard! Ohhhhh!" then her body quivered and shuddered as she experienced the orgasm. I was right behind her, and shot a load of cum into her, groaning loudly with spasm after spasm shaking me.

We stopped after a moment, with me gently fondling her boobs as she caressed my neck and ran her fingers through my hair. We slowly came to our senses, and I realized I had a dripping wet female on top of my jacket on a table in my squadron, and we had both just come in a big way. We looked at each other. She was grinning.

"That's not what I expected this evening to turn into!"

I had to agree. "You'll have to visit more often."

She kissed me. "You may have an idea there, Sergeant. Now help me find something to clean up with. I'm a sticky mess!"

The only thing I had on me was a handkerchief in a pocket, which I shared but could tell it was not up to the task. I pulled out and went to the men's latrine in search of toilet paper and maybe some paper towels. I brought those back, and after wiping each other off, we pulled our pants and underwear up and I zipped up my flight suit, now looking halfway respectable. With a smile on her face, we walked out to her car.

I said, "We can go back into the viz center, or ..."

She laughed and said, "No, Dirk, We are very disheveled and anyone that looks at us will know what we have been up to. I'll go home now and call you at the facility later after I clean up. That was an interesting evening."

BIG GIRLS NEED LOVE, TOO! BARBARA FROM KOKOMO 63

We kissed again, and she got into her car and left as I got into the cold government truck and went back to my home away from home.

Short Notice Trip

Back at the alert facility, I was paged for a phone call just before 10 pm. Barb was all set at home.

She said, "I'm curled up on the sofa under a blanket with a glass of wine. I wish you were here."

"Barb, in a perfect world I would be. You know I wanted to spend tonight with you."

"I know. If you were here, we would be having sex again by now. Not that I feel neglected after you took care of me tonight."

I had to laugh. "What the hell was that about anyway? We went from holding hands on the couch to you getting horny in about a minute and a half."

It was her turn to laugh. "I don't know! We were all romantic like a couple, and then I decided to put my hand on your leg, then I felt an urge come over me. I thought about us doing it at your trailer, and I guess that got me hot and bothered. Are you complaining?"

"Not at all! I was flattered that you got turned on. I'm glad we were able to take care of the need, although I admit that the venue was not very romantic. It was incredibly hot, though. It was the first time for me for something like that."

She laughed again. "Me, too." Then she took on a serious tone. "Dirk, we never finished the discussion. Where are we going with this? Are we just friends having sex, or something more?"

Uh, oh. This took a serious turn quickly. "I'm happy to be friends that have sex together and enjoy each other's company. As I said, I am not ready for anything long-term. I really enjoy being romantic with you, but if that's sending the wrong signals, let me know."

She sighed audibly. "I like playing girlfriend and all the things that come with that. Kissing, hugging, holding hands, talking sweetly, going on dates. I love sex with you, as you may have noticed. Can we keep things the way they are right now? We can see each other every now and then, be romantic during dates but not have fantasies about falling in love? I should say try not to have love fantasies, it's hard."

That sounded perfect to me. "I'd like that, Barb."

"Okay, it's settled then. I'm glad we talked about it. I had meant to talk about it in person tonight, but ... you know what happened. Oh! I forgot to give you your keys back."

I smiled into the phone. "You'll just have to come visit me tomorrow."

She giggled. "While tempting, and the thought of doing it on that table again immediately came to mind, I'm picking up my son in the morning. How about you come by my office Monday?"

"I can do that."

We talked for a minute more, then rang off. I sat for a minute, contemplating. She had come to realize that we would not be getting into a long-term relationship, and still wanted to date. I thought that turned out just like I had in mind.

In my dorm room downstairs, my roommate was still up reading, and after chatting for a minute, I hung up the flight jacket that I had been carrying around with me since I got back. There I noticed a stain on the inside of the jacket lining. Oh, no! This was a souvenir of the wild sex session on the table. I took it to the latrine and tried to wipe it down with a wet cloth. The goo came off, but there was a permanent stain. That stain was visible for the rest of the time I had the jacket, for years to come, and survived several trips to the dry cleaners. Each time I noticed it, I smiled.

I picked up my keys on Monday, with Barb's coworker watching intently. Barb was in a good mood, and I felt like we were in a good place. I had two days off and would go right back on alert with my crew on Thursday. We did not set any dates but loosely agreed to see each other when I got off my alert tour.

After starting my alert shift, I went over to the wing scheduling office and looked at the long-range schedule, searching out any possible good deals, when one of the schedulers took notice.

"Caldwell, we need a boom operator to fill in for a guy that got injured yesterday. It would mean a 30-day trip to England, leaving the Monday after your alert tour. Are you interested?"

"Hell, yes! Sign me up!"

He nodded. "I'll call your operations officer and propose it. It would mean you would have to out process and get ready for the trip while you are on alert."

"I'm willing to do that."

I raced over to the squadron and was standing there when the ops officer hung up the phone with scheduling. He had approved the trip and told me to get started on out processing. I got the checklist from my administrative section, then thought about Barb. I called her at her office.

"Hey, Barb. Want to meet for lunch at the NCO Club?"

She was in a good mood. "Sure, and then go by your trailer for a quickie?"

"That sounds very good to me, but I can't leave the base and you know it, you tease."

She laughed. "Poor Dirk. See you at noon?"

We met, and during lunch, I told her about my short-notice trip. She thought for a minute.

"That means after this weekend, I won't see you for a month?"

"That's right."

She took my hand across the table. "Dirk, this weekend I am going to Indianapolis with my Mom and Sister. I'm sorry, but we've had this planned for a while."

"I totally understand. I'll see you for sure when I get back, and it will be nicer weather in the spring, anyway."

As we ate, I toyed with the idea of inviting her over Thursday night after work for some sex but wanted her to come up with that on her own. She did not, so I kept my mouth shut, kissed her goodbye in the parking lot, and told her I'd see her in about a month.

I had a great trip to England, even meeting an English girl and having some fun with her, which should be its own short story. After returning, Barb and I had trouble getting together, although we had lunch a few times on base. I wondered if she was seeing someone else, which was fine with me if she was.

Summer rolled in with a vengeance, and I got to experience the Midwest during the hot weather. It was awful, except for some fun trips to the local lake camping with my friend Jim. He and Diane had a new baby girl as a result of that time I relieved him on alert. Diane kept trying to fix me up with one of her single friends, but that never worked out.

Then one day I met Gabriella and that started a whirlwind of events that took up the entire summer and fall. Things calmed down as the weather cooled off, and one day out of the blue Barb called me and wanted to go to lunch.

We met at the door, and I kissed her like it was old times, which she enjoyed. Over lunch, she said, "Word around the base is that you've been dating an Italian supermodel," she said teasingly.

"Aw, Barb. That's an example of how rumors get started. She isn't a supermodel, she's an advertising executive up in Chicago."

Barb looked at me across the table. "Are you still seeing her?"

I felt a bit uncomfortable. "Yes, now and then, nothing steady. She's traveling a lot this fall."

She was still looking at me. "So, you have some free time on your hands for local girls?"

This was going somewhere fast. "Yes, I suppose I do."

BIG GIRLS NEED LOVE, TOO! BARBARA FROM KOKOMO 69

She smiled. "I have a proposition for you. I'd like to invite you to go away with me for a long weekend. Somewhere there is a nice resort. We can get reacquainted and have a long, serious talk about us."

"Us?" was all I could say.

"Yes, whether or not we will continue to be friends that date, or something more."

"Aw, Barb, I'm still not wanting to have a committed relationship. That hasn't changed at all during the summer."

"I know, Dirk. This is more for me, to see if I can handle dating an Air Force guy that gets pulled away for duty whenever they need you. It may help me shape the way I think about you, and other things."

"Well, I guess we could do that. I'd enjoy seeing you again."

She smiled. "Do you mean you would enjoy having sex with me again?"

She had me there. "That is part of seeing you, so yes."

We compared schedules and came up with a mutually agreeable date for that weekend. She left with a big smile on her face, saying she would make all the arrangements. I went back to the squadron and was stopped in the hallway by the Chief.

"Caldwell, I just came from the ops officer. We just got tasked with a short-notice trip to Florida to support some real-world reconnaissance missions. Your crew is assigned as primary. You'll leave tomorrow and be gone for a week."

My heart sank. This was just after I told Barb I could go away with her. I pleaded my case with the Chief. He wasn't buying it.

"Sergeant, this is the military. We assign you tasks based on our best judgment of your skills and training and the needs of the service, and in turn, it is your responsibility to accomplish those assignments to the best of your professional ability without complaining. Is there an issue with that?"

"Just my personal life, Chief."

He shook his head. "A woman that understands and helps support our crazy life is to be treasured. Ones that don't will make your life miserable." He walked away, shaking his head. He was right.

I called Barb at her office right away. "Don't make those plans yet. Something came up. Can you meet me for a drink after work to talk about it?"

She was furious. "Something came up in the hour since we talked? Did you get a better offer, Dirk? Did your supermodel girlfriend call and want you to come to Chicago?"

It was not the right time to explain again that Gabby was not a supermodel. "No, Barb, it's a military trip, and ..."

"I've heard enough, Dirk. I think we are done seeing each other. Goodbye."

With that, she hung up. She had a right to be ticked off, but I wondered if she would ever understand the life I had committed to. I felt pretty low for disappointing Barb but may have learned something valuable about her and women. My crew was gathering in my favorite mission planning room, and I joined them to prepare for the trip to Florida.

An interesting turn of events

The fall turned colder, and things were happening for me. I moved out of my crappy trailer and into a nice apartment in Kokomo. Gabby came down from Chicago and helped me furnish and decorate it. It was a hit with my girlfriends, except Barb, who had not seen it. She was still not speaking to me. I got some nicer clothes, better music, and was looking at a new car. My confidence with women had skyrocketed, and I learned a lot from Gabby which helped my sex life. Things were going very well.

Barb called me unexpectedly and wanted to meet for a drink after work at the club. I could not imagine what this would be about since she had been mad at me for months, but she said it was important and could not wait. Maybe she wanted to get together. I would find out soon enough.

I was at the club at the appointed time, wearing my newer clothes, which were a navy blazer over grey slacks and a long-sleeved pale blue shirt. I had fashionable loafers on with stylish socks. For an Air Force Staff Sergeant, I was looking pretty spiffy. She arrived almost on time, and we got a table away from others where we could talk in private. She had noticed my clothes and commented. "You look nice, Dirk."

"Thanks."

We looked at each other in silence. It was her idea to meet, I would wait all night if I had to for her to initiate the conversation. Finally, she started.

"I imagine you are wondering why I wanted to talk after all this time."

I just nodded. I was going to let her talk it out.

"Dirk, I've done something stupid."

I waited.

"I was out last night with my friends and my Mom, and I got a little drunk."

I finally said, "No crime in that, as long as you don't drive."

She went on, "No, it's what I talked about. They were teasing me about not getting any sex since you and I were not seeing each other."

She hesitated and took a gulp of her drink. Liquid courage. I waited.

"Then I told them that was right and how I was sure missing it, and how you and I had the best sex that I'd ever had. About how you could make me come multiple times, and you know … could do me hard when I wanted it that way."

Oh, my goodness. Where was this headed? I was looking at her straight in the eyes.

"And what else, Barb?"

"And then they teased me some more, and asked if they could call you since I wasn't going to see you anymore."

I could not believe this. "And then what?"

Her words came in a rush. "So, I said they could call you and gave them your phone number. They said they could not wait to call you and make a date so they could see what I was talking about."

I was getting pretty pissed off. "So, you gave your girlfriends my phone number and gave them your blessing to have sex with me? Is that it?"

She was not done. "That's not all, Dirk. One of them was my mother."

I was floored. My voice involuntarily raised several decibels. "Your mother is going to call me for sex? Are you fucking insane?"

Barb buried her face in her hands. "Oh, Dirk. I'm so ashamed. I don't know what to do."

I sat for a minute, absolutely stunned. "Here's what you're going to do. Call your mother and tell her that you changed your mind, that I'm not going to be passed around to her or your friends as a consolation prize just because you don't want to see me anymore."

She was crying. "I'm so sorry! I'll talk to them, but they were so interested and excited about meeting you … I don't know if I can turn that off. It may make it worse!"

"Well, Barb. Here's what I'm going to do. If any of them call me, I will meet with them and explain that while you and I were friends, that does not give them the key to Dirk's stud service."

She was sniffling. "I guess I deserve that. You said we were friends, like used to be."

I was furious. "Do you think we are still friends after this?"

Crying again, she said, "No, I don't think so. I blabbed about our private experiences and violated your trust."

I was starting to calm down a little. "I mean we did not swear a privacy pledge or anything, but that's just common sense, Barb."

"You're right, Dirk. I made a mistake, and I'm sorry.

I reached across and took her hand. "I accept your apology."

A wan smile came across her face. She blew her nose and sat up straighter.

"Thank you. I'm sorry to put you in this position."

Trying to make light of the situation, I said, "And who knows, some of your friends may work out and be great sex partners."

"Even my Mom?"

I was still feeling a little pissed off, and out of spite, I said, "I don't know about that, Barb. What do you think? Should I have sex with your Mom?"

She shook her head. "She'll chicken out, there is no way she'll call you."

I wanted to push the point home. "But if she does, is it okay with you if I have sex with your Mom?"

She looked defiant. "If she calls you and you find her attractive, go for it."

I had never had a conversation like this in my life. I drained my drink and took a deep breath, then let it out, feeling the anger leave me.

"Shall we have another drink and talk about something else, as old friends do?"

She tried to smile. "I'd like another drink with my old friend."

We sat together for a while, trying to talk about everything but me having sex with her Mom. To say it was awkward would be an understatement.

Meeting her Mom

I thought about what Barb and I had talked about on the way home. Crazy. The more I thought about it, I realized that I did not mind a referral to her girlfriends, as long as they wanted sex only and not a relationship. That sounded kind of cool the more I thought about it. What a crazy world.

I had just walked into the apartment when the phone rang.

A woman's voice. "Hello, is this Dirk?"

"Yes, it is, who's calling?"

She hesitated. "This is Jean. Ah ... Barb's mother."

I did not skip a beat. "Hello, Jean. How are you?"

"I'm fine, Dirk."

There was an awkward pause.

"What can I do for you, Jean?"

"I ah ... wanted to talk to you." She was nervous as hell. I was not making it any easier on her.

"Sure, Jean. What would you like to talk about?"

She tried to stall. "Have you talked to Barbara recently?"

"Yes, as a matter of fact, she and I had drinks tonight."

"Oh, I see. And did she tell you that ... I might call?"

"Yes, she did, Jean."

"Well, I'd like to set up a meeting. You know, to get to know you."

"That's fine, Jean. Let's see, today is Thursday. What are you doing Saturday? How about 4 pm at the Holiday Inn in Kokomo? They have a nice lounge where we could talk over a drink."

She sounded relieved. "That would be fine, Dirk. I'll see you then."

I got her number in case something came up, and we rang off. I laughed to myself. Jean was going to either not show up or show up and then not be able to go through with it. I wasn't doing anything else Saturday. I might as well have some fun with Barb's Mom.

Saturday came, and I dressed in my date outfit and got to the Holiday Inn on time. I realized I had no idea what Jean looked like. Maybe she would recognize me. I probably should have worked that out beforehand. Would she be big, like Barb? So many unanswered questions, soon to be resolved.

There was a nice-looking lady about the right age waiting in the lobby. We made eye contact, and she asked, "Dirk?"

I walked up to her with my hand out. "Hello, Jean. It's nice to meet you."

Her hand was moist. Nerves, I suppose. I mean, who wouldn't be nervous about meeting a man half her age and setting up a tryst?

"Nice to meet you, Dirk. I've heard a lot about you." That was an automatic response, then she blushed when she realized that it could be construed, "Man, you have some reputation for satisfying women in the sack!"

I smiled. "Shall we go in?"

We entered the sparsely populated lounge and selected a table in a dim corner, suitable for private, sexy conversation. I looked at her. "This is out of the way; we should have some privacy here." She nodded assent.

A bored looking waitress came over, and we ordered. I got a scotch and soda; she got red wine. I waited for her to say something. I decided to give her a break and start us out.

"Jean, why don't you tell me about yourself?"

She described where she lived and worked and volunteered that she and Barb's Dad had been divorced for some time, and she lived alone. There were two other daughters and a smattering of grandkids.

I said, "Now, Jean. You don't look old enough to have grandkids."

She smiled. "I hear that a lot. I'm 57."

I did not reveal that I was now just 26. I had been looking her over as she talked. She was a nice looking petite lady, about five foot five inches tall, and had dyed blondish hair in a fashionable short coiffure.

Her face had some lines on the cheeks and forehead, with the start of crow's feet at the corners of the eyes. Her face was not round, just beginning to get a little flesh on it. Her brown eyes had tasteful eye shadow and eyeliner applied. There was some extra flesh under the chin, and some on her neck. Her shoulders were straight, and she had good posture. She wore a nice suit with a matching jacket and skirt. The white blouse was visible, with a gold necklace. She had stylish, medium-sized dangly earrings in pierced ears. Her chest looked like her boobs were of a good size, and the jacket hid her tummy, so I could not assess that right now. Her hands had some veins protruding, and some age spots. Her fingernails were painted, with a fashionable ring on her right hand. When she had walked in ahead of me, her backside was a little broad, but not too large. The legs that I could see looked fine. She wore conservative shoes with a low heel. She looked like an account manager at a bank, which she was. She looked nothing at all like her daughter.

While not seeming nervous as she spoke, she was going at the wine pretty quickly as we chatted. We ordered a second round, and then I decided to cut to the chase.

"Jean, what was it you wanted to see me about?"

She was surprised. "I, ah ... thought that ... we could ... make a date."

I smiled kindly. "You mean a date like this, Jean?"

"Well, no. I'm sorry. This is harder than I thought it would be."

"Go ahead, Jean. Take your time."

"After hearing about you from Barb ..."

I pushed her. "Hearing what about me from Barb, Jean?"

"You know. The way you ... treat women."

I decided to help her out. "You mean the way I have sex with women, Jean?"

She took a gulp of her wine. "Yes, that's it."

"And you wanted to make a date and find out about that, to check out what Barb told you girls and see if it was true? To have sex and see if it was satisfying?"

She was blushing now. I was hitting her hard. Well, she should be blushing.

"Yes, Dirk. I found that idea very exciting. And now I am here with you. It's not something I would normally do."

I smiled at her. "What do you think, Jean? Are you attracted to me?"

She looked me straight in the eyes, and I immediately felt bad about the way I had been talking to her.

"Yes, Dirk. I find that I have a strong attraction to you."

"Strong enough to have sex with me, even though I am much younger than you and you just met me?"

She was still looking me in the eyes and had a simple, unequivocal answer. "Yes."

Good enough for me. I took her hand and held it, stroking the flesh between the thumb and forefinger with my thumb. She was looking at me intently. It was time to find out.

"Kiss me, Jean. We have to find out if there's an attraction."

We were sitting close together. She hesitated for a moment, then leaned over and gave me a closed mouth kiss. She held it for a few seconds, then backed up. Our noses were about an inch apart. She was staring into my eyes. I held her hand. Time stood still. Then she leaned in again and this time, it was a full-up, tongue-searching, hello there kiss. Our tongues intertwined hungrily. She was a good kisser. It was fun and arousing. After about 15 seconds of that, she backed off again, still looking into my eyes. Her hand came up and went behind my neck, pulling me to her for another deep kiss that lasted at least 30 seconds. She released me, and we both sat back, smiling.

I said, "You're a great kisser. I think we may have an attraction going."

She was smiling. "I think we do."

I took her hand and placed it on top of mine. "Just one more thing. You have control of my hand now. Place it where you want me to touch you."

She took a quick look around. There was nobody anywhere near us, and nobody watching us. She moved my hand off the table, pulled it under her skirt, and onto her crotch to hold it firmly against her panties. Her eyes were locked with mine. I used the opportunity to trace her labia with my fingers, feeling them through the damp underwear. Her eyes closed, and her lips parted as she enjoyed the sensation.

After a couple of moments, she released my hand, and reluctantly I pulled it out from under her skirt. Her eyes opened, and she stared at me intently.

I asked her, "Are you getting wet down there?"

She nodded.

"Are your nipples erect?"

Another nod.

Another question. "Do you want me right now?"

She nodded and answered with a husky whisper. "Yes, I do. Right now."

I smiled and attracted the attention of the waitress. "First, we will share a dessert."

Jean looked at me quizzically. She had just put my hand on her pussy indicating her ready status and had told me her nipples were standing at attention and her pussy was wet with desire, and now I was getting something to eat. What the hell?

I tried to satisfy her curiosity. "My friend says that lovers should always share dessert before making love."

She smiled again, "Are we going to be lovers, Dirk?"

I smiled at her and borrowed a line from Gabriella. "Yes. We will make love soon."

The End

To read more about Dirk and Jean's encounter, please try my novel:
To All the Girls I've Loved Before: Sexy Short Stories Book 1
https://www.draft2digital.com/catalog/1272260

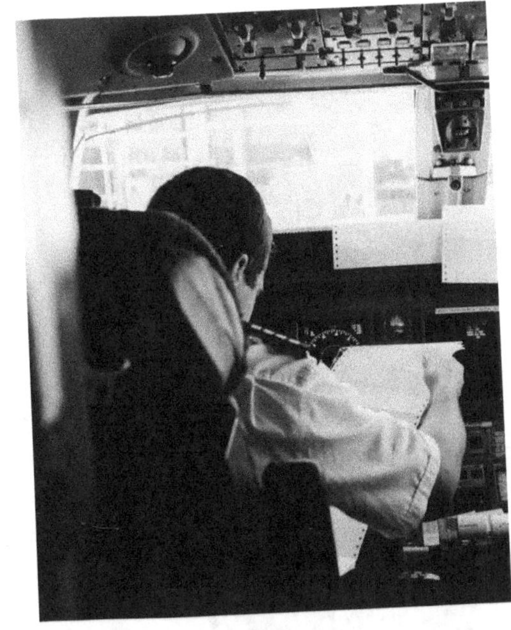

About the Author

Dirk Caldwell is the pen name of the author of an erotic book series. Dirk embodies the life experiences of the author as an Air Force veteran and commercial airline pilot. Most of the content is true and relates to the author's experiences. It's up to the reader to decide what is fiction and what is true life.

Don't miss out!

Visit the website below and you can sign up to receive emails whenever Dirk Caldwell publishes a new book. There's no charge and no obligation.

https://books2read.com/r/B-A-UHDZ-CHUMC

BOOKS 2 READ

Connecting independent readers to independent writers.

Did you love *Big Girls Need Love, too! Barbara from Kokomo*? T̶ you should read *A Night in Eufaula with Lynn*[1] by Dirk Caldw

Air Force enlisted man Dirk travels to rural Oklahoma for a da the lake that does not work out. He then runs across small tow grocery store clerk Lynn, and they arrange to meet. Dirk dis that Lynn has many unsatisfied desires that she is very aggressive getting resolved, and the result is a night of hot action beyond wildest expectations. Lynn knows what she wants and is very about getting it! The author describes the non-stop action in e detail, bringing the reader into the room as the action takes pl won't want to miss this latest steamy installment of Dirk's adv Read the sample!

1. https://books2read.com/u/4EEnno

2. https://books2read.com/u/4EEnno